Living Victoriously

in

The Last Days

by
Brian Reddish

Living Victoriously in The Last Days
© 2018 by Brian Reddish
ISBN 978-0-9934887-9-5
Published by Caracal Books
United Kingdom www.facebook.com/CaracalBooks/

The internet addresses, email addresses, and phone numbers in this book are accurate at the time of publication.

Cover photo: www.shutterstock.com/Dorottya Mathe

A Word from the Author

At the beginning of 2017, my pastor gave me four dates, spread throughout the year, upon which to preach at the Ambassadors Bible Church in Watchfield, Oxfordshire, where I and my wife attend.

Upon entering the New Year that January, and whilst thinking about the task in hand, I felt moved by God to consider the days and times we were living in. The Word that I was to preach had to be relevant and not just a "good sermon!"

God put a theme into my mind. The theme that came to me vividly was:

Living in The Last Days!

I had been taught much upon this topic many years previously and what came to mind was a verse we used as a title to those studies some 35 years ago! It is found at the beginning of the Book of Hebrews, Chapter 1 and verses 1-2:

God, who at various times and in various ways spoke in time past to the fathers by the prophets, **has in these last days spoken to us by His Son.**

This was, if you like, God's supreme revelation to man, and the very mention of the phrase "Last Days" speaks of a sense of finality. This is it! God has not spoken by mortal man anymore, but **God has spoken by His Son – Jesus Christ!**

This gave me great impetus to open up the Bible and declare exactly what God has spoken to us about and, in particular, what these "Last days" reveal to us.

I knew I could easily spend four sermons preaching upon this topic! It didn't take too long to come upon a main point and general theme for my sermons:

- What does the Bible say it will be like during the Last days?

- How does the Bible teach us to live in the last days?

What I did not realize at the time was that I would be writing this book containing all of my findings!

How to Read this Book

Each day's reading is fairly extensive and focuses around a particular point. It may be useful to consider reading it in two parts; for example, one in the morning and the other in the evening.

All passages of Scriptures are given in full and are taken from the Spirit Filled Life, New King James Bible. This, I thought, would enable the reader to flow through the text without looking up the Bible passages themselves. Even so, it would be a good idea to locate each quoted scripture in the Bible at some stage so as to understand the context in which it is given.

May God Himself richly bless you in reading through this book. I pray for you to be taught by Him, prepared by His Word and enlightened by His Holy Spirit so that, together with the supernatural ability and power of the Holy Spirit, you will be able to live an over-

overcoming life of victory through all the battles that lie
ahead — that we all must face.

Brian Reddish
December 2017

Day by Day Topical Index

PART 1

DAY 1

The Last Days — God's Promise of Old

*God, who at various times and in various ways spoke in time past to the fathers by the prophets, has, in these **last days**, spoken to us by His Son...*   Hebrews:1: 1-2

There is a sense of finality about the words "last days" mentioned here right at the beginning of the book of Hebrews. The writer in this statement refers to God's involvement in history — from days long ago when He spoke to individuals, to a people, to a nation by the prophets — but now God has spoken to the world through His Son, Jesus Christ. No longer does God speak just to a privileged nation, Israel; now, everyone is included — you and me, too.

Suddenly, there is a choice to be made. The fact that God "has spoken" automatically brings with it a challenge — the message that God has spoken of and conveyed to us — and all because of what Jesus has achieved for every individual on the cross! The implication demands even greater attention regarding what has been spoken, seeing as it is His Son Who speaks, or more precisely it is God speaking directly to the whole human race through His Son!

The text says that previously God 'had spoken in various ways,' and this can be observed in the Scriptures. For example, the Bible records instances where God communicated to man by dreams, visions, angels, a burning bush and through direct speech, which was mostly but not exclusively to men of God referred to as *prophets*. The message was largely directed in those days to His chosen people. To Abraham, Isaac and Jacob;

Then, to their offspring until a nation was created directly by God—His chosen people through whom all families of the earth would be blessed through their Messiah, the Lord Jesus Christ. This was God's assurance to Abraham found in Genesis 12:3. Such is the relevance and importance of this promise that it is well worth mentioning the whole context of the passage where this promise made to the first Patriarch, Abraham, is recorded.

> *I will make you [Abraham] a great nation;*
> *I will bless you*
> *And make your name great;*
> *And you shall be a blessing.*
> *I will bless those who bless you,*
> *And I will curse him who curses you;*
> **And in you all the families of the earth shall be blessed**. Genesis 12: 2-3

Here we see how God separated Abraham from his idolatrous family to make him and his descendants the messianic nation that would bring salvation to all Earth's families—through Jesus, the Christ! The promise is a declaration by God Himself, and the language used is worth taking heed of! Israel is the only nation that has been created directly by God so as to fulfil His purposes, and this was achieved and fulfilled when Jesus was born of the Holy Spirit in a manger in Bethlehem, lived thirty-three years and died on a cross to pay the price for the sins of the whole world!

Peter, in the Acts of the Apostles, Chapter 3 verses 22–25, referred to this very Scripture when he was preaching to Jews:

For Moses truly said to the fathers, 'The Lord your God will raise up for you a Prophet like me from your brethren. Him you shall hear in all things whatever He says to you…' Yes, and all the prophets from Samuel and those who follow, as many as have spoken, have also foretold these days. You are sons of the prophets and of the covenant which God made with our fathers, saying to Abraham, 'And in your seed all the families of the earth shall be blessed.'

And so, this climax of history and God's visitation has been and gone, although the victorious work accomplished will live on for all eternity! Jesus Christ, God's Son, came into this world, and as a faithful witness, He spoke of His Father and the Kingdom of God, offering salvation to all men who would repent and believe the Gospel (*good news!*) thereby receiving God's gift, purchased through His Own Blood on the cross.

Interestingly, Jesus' ministry was heralded in by someone who He called the greatest of all prophets, John the Baptist—great because he had been designated the task of preparing the way of the Lord!

So, God was made flesh and dwelt among us (John 1: 14) as promised. In other words, God has visited us and spoken to us through His Son in what is now termed **the last days!**

LIFE APPLICATIONS

- Let us take to heart all of God's promises in His Word and be assured that what He has said will come to fruition!

- Acknowledge today that you can become a child of God because of what Jesus has done for you upon the cross. There is access for everyone who comes to God through Jesus, and it is only by this gift of grace that anyone can be saved.

DAY 2

The Last Days — God's Timeline

God is eternal. He is without beginning and without end, from everlasting to everlasting! This is a difficult concept to our natural mind but one, nevertheless, that the Bible teaches and which we can receive, accept and benefit from. A favourite Scripture of mine is found in Micah 5:2 and reads:

> *But you, Bethlehem Ephrathah, Though you are little among the thousands of Judah, Yet out of you shall come forth to Me The One to be Ruler in Israel, Whose goings forth are from of old, **From everlasting**.* (Literally, from the days of eternity.)

Bethlehem means 'House of Bread,' and many Jews at the time of Christ saw this passage as messianic and believed that the Messiah would be born in Bethlehem. The word 'Ephrathah' is synonymous with that of the county or region within which a town lies.

God dwells in eternity and not in time. If you like, time is part of God's creation; it has a beginning and it has an end. The sun and moon determine our time; we define a year as the period it takes for the earth to travel around the sun, whereas the time taken for the moon to orbit the earth is aptly called one month. Thus, God defined day and night. It is the external bodies of the sun and moon which He created and put in place that determine our time! We did not invent it; God did!

> *Then God said, 'Let there be lights in the firmament of the heavens to divide the day from the night; and let them*

be for signs and seasons, and for days and years;'
Genesis1:14

Since time is a creation of God, one could think of it as a very long piece of string with a beginning and an end. The beginning of the string represents creation — when time began — whilst the end of the string represents the end of time. The phrases **latter days** or **last days** are terms used widely in the Bible and refer to the days leading up to the end of time. The days following the climax of history — Christ's death and resurrection — are termed **the last days,** and these extend from His resurrection to when He comes again, the Second Coming! Our passage of Scripture from Hebrews Chapter 1: 1-2 declares the beginning of the last days when it says:

God… has in these last days spoken to us by His Son.

The coming of Jesus brought about the beginning of the end. God had spoken many times throughout history —

…but now, once at the end of the ages, He has appeared to put away sin by the sacrifice of Himself.   Hebrews 9:26

It was the superiority of Christ, the Son of God, above all others who came before Him, that made the difference. The message He brought was far greater, and He did not come just to speak to an individual, a people or a nation, but to the whole world. The Bible says that God was in Christ reconciling the world to Himself (2 Corinthians 5:19).

Because of the superior message that has been faithfully delivered to the world, we are warned of complacency regarding what Jesus has declared openly to all!

Therefore we must give the more earnest heed to the things we have heard, lest we drift away. Hebrews 2:1

[H]ow shall we escape if we neglect so great a salvation, which at the first began to be spoken by the Lord… Hebrews 2:3

Believers are to take heed lest adverse doctrines sweep them away from their Christian convictions like a drifting ship taken past its safe port of call by the changing winds of the world and deviousness of false teaching through the cunning and craftiness of men.

[T]hat we should no longer be children, tossed to and fro and carried about with every wind of doctrine, by the trickery of men… Ephesians 4:14

In the last days, it shall increasingly become necessary to contend for the faith as pointed out in Jude 3:

Beloved, while I was very diligent to write to you concerning our common salvation, I found it necessary to write to you exhorting you to contend earnestly for the faith which was once for all delivered to the saints.

We shall address this later when we look at what the Bible says about the conditions in the world in the last days and how God's people ought to live.

We rest assured therefore that God in Christ has spoken to us in these last days; and as we apply our faith to what He tells us, so we shall discover the victorious life that He promises that will take us from this world and into the next!

LIFE APPLICATIONS

- What do you consider to be the most important thing in your life?

- How does the fact that you are living in the last days affect your attitude and choices?

- Do you ever think about Christ's coming?

DAY 3

The Last Days — God's Everlasting Love

The Lord has appeared of old to me, saying: 'Yes, I have loved you with an everlasting love; Therefore with lovingkindness I have drawn you.' Jeremiah 31:3

"Of old" literally means *from afar*; in fact, we might just add *from eternity,* as this fits the context very well!

Here we read that God has loved us with an everlasting love, and we see an incredible, amazing word regarding His love — from *everlasting*! Yes, He loves me with an *everlasting* love! How can that be seeing as I have only been alive a few years and did not even exist before that? This requires some thought by examining the Scriptures.

On Day 2 we read:

But you, Bethlehem Ephrathah, Though you are little among the thousands of Judah, Yet out of you shall come forth to Me The One to be Ruler in Israel, Whose goings forth are from of old, From **everlasting.**

Here we see that Jesus was there with God in Eternity before anything was made — that is, from everlasting — and it is interesting that in our Scripture for this session, God's love is said to be from everlasting too! Could it be that God, in Christ, loved us way back then and knew about us before we were born? The answer is YES! Whilst that may sound incredible and perhaps difficult to understand, the Bible declares this truth throughout its pages!

[J]ust as He chose us in Him before the foundation of the world, that we should be holy and without blame before Him in love,   Ephesians 1:4

God's plan in the beginning was to have a family. He created mankind in His own image and in type and similitude to His Eternal Son, and this He planned back in eternity. The above Scripture in Ephesians tells us that we were chosen in Him before the foundation of the world that we should be holy and without blame before Him in love. However, God foresaw everything that would happen to man before He created him. Remember the long piece of string in Session 2 that represented time? God could look down from eternity and see the end from the beginning of His creation. He saw exactly the way things would turn out, even taking into account man's free will and freedom of choice! Consequently, it was planned back in eternity for Jesus to come into the world and be crucified to save mankind from their sin.

In Ephesians 1:4 it declares that God chose us in Him **before** the foundation of the world — that is before creation and before sin came into existence. When God had made all things and man had sinned, His plan in sending Christ our Saviour was finally called into being. Then and only then was it necessary for Christ to come and die to pay the penalty for our sin. God was not taken by surprise; He had foreseen it and had already planned for it! The following Scriptures make this very clear.

Revelation 13:8 says that Christ was slain '*from the foundation of the world*' as opposed to **before** the foundation of the world. In other words, after the fall,

God's plan to send Christ was effectively brought into being.

God knows the hearts of all people in every generation, and He foresaw those who would believe in Him, knowing even before the world began those whose names would be written in the Lamb's book of life! Further, in 1 Peter 1:20-21, it reads:

He indeed was foreordained before the foundation of the world, but was manifest in these last times for you who through Him believe in God, who raised Him from the dead and gave Him glory, so that your faith and hope are in God.

Now, the scripture in Jeremiah — *Yes, I have loved you with an **everlasting** love* – seems to take on a new meaning! The word *everlasting* is only usually used regarding God and is therefore very special whenever it is applied to us mortals! Remember John 3:16?

*For God so loved the world that He gave His only begotten Son, that whoever believes in Him should not perish but have **everlasting** life.*

We do not know who will be saved in that day; instead we are commissioned to go into all the world and preach the Gospel to everyone — and ***whoever*** believes shall be saved. Therefore, we have no idea who God is able to save! We must love and treat everyone equally as someone who God can save whatever we might think regarding the outward appearance. God has shown us some idea though of the type of person He specifically chooses, and it's not who we might think at first sight!

For you see your calling, brethren, that not many wise according to the flesh, not many mighty, not many noble, are called. But God has chosen the foolish things of the world to put to shame the wise, and God has chosen the weak things of the world to put to shame the things which are mighty; and the base things of the world and the things which are despised God has chosen; and the things which are not, to bring to nothing the things that are, that no flesh should glory in His presence.

1 Corinthians 1:26-29

LIFE APPLICATIONS

- How much time do you give considering eternal things given that we only live several decades?

- Even though we know that life in this world is only temporary, do we commit ourselves to serving God and living for Him in light of this?

- Why do you think it is that some people still turn their backs upon God in spite of knowing their lives are short in this world and that one day they will have to stand before Him?

DAY 4

The Last Days — How Long Are They?

The last days in time have been ticking away for over two thousand years, and we are still here! Has God forgotten? Not at all! One day with the Lord is as a thousand years and a thousand years as one day! The fact is, we don't know how long the last days will be. It is like saying, 'When will Jesus come again?' We are simply given signs to look out for and warnings to be aware of. Remember the words of Jesus to His disciples when they enquired about the end times?

And He said to them, 'It is not for you to know times or seasons which the Father has put in His own authority. But you shall receive power when the Holy Spirit has come upon you; and you shall be witnesses to Me in Jerusalem, and in all Judea and Samaria, and to the end of the earth."   Acts 1: 7-8

In other words, Jesus was saying, "I want you to focus upon the job at hand — to reach the lost."

God's focus is upon the salvation of souls for His Eternal Kingdom. He is not willing for any to perish, but even so the Bible says:

For yet a little while, And He who is coming will come and will not tarry.   Hebrews 10:37

The passage below in 2 Peter 3:9 is worth a look, for it declares that some people will doubt the coming of the Lord.

The lord is not slack concerning His promise, as some

count slackness, but is longsuffering toward us, not willing that any should perish but that all should come to repentance.

It is often said that God hates sin but loves the sinner. The Bible says God has no pleasure in the death of the wicked but encourages all to come to Him.

Let the wicked forsake his way, And the unrighteous man his thoughts; Let him return to the Lord... For He will abundantly pardon. Isaiah 55:7

In fact, the greatest encourager in the universe is God who calls fallen mankind, all of whom are born sinners by nature and not just by deed.

[F]or all have sinned and fall short of the glory of God, Romans 3: 23

And further,

There is none righteous, no, not one. Romans 3:10

A heart-warming example of God graciously reaching out to His fallen people of old is found in Isaiah 1: 18.

'Come now, and let us reason together,' Says the Lord. 'Though your sins are like scarlet, They shall be white as snow; Though they are red like crimson, They shall be as wool.'

Each person must choose for themselves; that is, God has given man prerogative or free will. It is therefore imperative that we make the right choices in life, for everyone is accountable to God, their Creator, to give an account of what they have done — in this matter there is no choice!

The Bible declares that God's love is long-suffering. God openly says that He has demonstrated His love towards us in that while we were yet sinners, Christ died for us. God looks upon the timeline of each of our individual lives, knowing the best time to act, and He gently provides opportunities for each one to hear and know His call upon their lives. It is a delicate matter, and only God has the tender love and patience to do this. But such is His everlasting love that He will never give up. One could, in turn, ask how patient and longsuffering we are with people.

Sometimes, the only way possible for God to save us is by permitting difficulties to happen in our lives — even sickness — and sometimes He might speak to us through the death of a friend or loved one so that we might come to the realization that we so desperately need to be saved by Him or face a lost eternity! Is it not worth a season of trouble for a time if the end result is that I make my peace with God to live eternally with Him forever thereafter? This is the raw truth of the matter! I must ultimately choose! God will never force me, though He will call me many times and seek to draw me with His mercy, love and grace.

A song writer once wrote —

Oh, the love that sought me!
Oh, the blood that bought me!

Oh, the grace that brought me to the fold
Wondrous grace that brought me to the fold.[i]

Again, another famous song sums it up—

Amazing grace, how sweet the sound that saved a wretch like me. I once was lost but now I'm found, was blind but now I see![ii]

That is why it is so important to hear God's Word. Faith comes by hearing and hearing by the Word of God. It is God's way that the preaching and teaching of His Word—together with the ministry of the Holy Spirit— has the power to open the eyes of the spiritually blind and reveal Who Jesus is! The power is great, because the victory Jesus wrought through His death upon the cross was great! We often say: there is power in the Blood of Jesus! It is the greatest power in the universe. Because God, our eternal father, has received the finished and complete work of His Son on the cross, He has now put Him in authority over all Heaven and Earth. In fact—

… for there is no other name under Heaven given among men by which we must be saved.   Acts 4: 12

Therefore, God also has highly exalted Him and given Him the name which is above every name, that at the name of Jesus every knee should bow, of those in heaven, and of those on earth, and of those under the earth, and that every tongue should confess that Jesus Christ is Lord, to the glory of God the Father.   Philippians 2: 9-11

LIFE APPLICATIONS

- God uses His people to reach the lost with His Word of truth and love; are you such a person?

- God loves all people, desiring them to be saved without respect of persons. Am I ever guilty of selecting only certain people to associate with or speak to—those I like—even though Jesus died for everyone?

- When was the last time I told someone about Jesus?

DAY 5

The Last Days — Being Ready!

But of that day and hour no one knows, not even the angels of heaven, but My Father only.   Matthew 24: 36

Watch therefore, for you do not know what hour your Lord is coming. But know this, that if the master of the house had known what hour the thief would come, he would have watched and not allowed his house to be broken into. Therefore you also be ready, for the Son of Man is coming at an hour you do not expect.   Matthew 24: 42-44

These Scriptures tell us emphatically that no one knows the time when Jesus will return, and according to Jesus, only His Father has this knowledge; so whatever men may say — and this most certainly includes all those who would speculate — do not believe them!

An important point, however, is that we are commanded to be ready for His unexpected coming! Each one of us must answer this requirement ourselves, for to be ready is a personal responsibility and no one else can tell us in its entirety what we must do to be ready to meet the Lord — either when He comes again or when He takes me individually. For example, it may be that there is some matter I must put right in my life, perhaps to make peace with someone who I may have offended. Clearly such things I should deal with straightaway. Even so, there are vitally important and essential things that apply to us all, without respect of persons. Most importantly and above all else, I must have turned to God to make my peace with Him at a definite time, asking His forgiveness for my sins.

As time goes on, our commitment to the Lord needs to progressively mature, and one short passage in the book of Romans will suffice to give every believer some important — but not exclusive — directions as to how:

I beseech you therefore, brethren, by the mercies of God, that you present your bodies a living sacrifice, holy, acceptable to God, which is your reasonable service. And do not be conformed to this world, but be transformed by the renewing of your mind, that you may prove what is that good and acceptable and perfect will of God.   Romans 12: 1-2

The above is a good and wise statement on how we should follow the Lord. With sound, balanced teaching, we should seek to follow in understanding every element of this passage of Scripture so that we progress in spirit, soul and body, remembering that our faith only works by love, and our personal relationship with the Lord always takes priority over all our giving, service and ministry.

Whilst it is necessary for a person to have come to the Lord through salvation, we are also instructed to come to Him daily, committing our lives to Him, confessing our sins, for the Bible says that:

If we confess our sins, He is faithful and just to forgive us our sins and to cleanse us from all unrighteousness.
1 John 1:9

We should pray regularly and study His Word. In this manner, we shall learn of Him and know more of His thoughts and ways as revealed and taught by the Holy Spirit so that, progressively, we can grow from glory to glory, becoming more like Christ.

We are continually learning to follow the Lord; it is progressive and, indeed, a life-long experience! Remember, God did not save us because we were righteous — *for there is none righteous, no not one* — so we should never take a self-righteous attitude but always submit ourselves to Him daily in humility and gratitude!

> *For by grace you have been saved through faith, and that not of yourselves; it is the gift of God, not of works, lest anyone should boast.*　　　　　Ephesians 2: 8-9

> *Beloved, now we are children of God; and it has not yet been revealed what we shall be, but we know that when He is revealed, we shall be like Him, for we shall see Him as He is. And everyone who has this hope in Him purifies himself, just as He is pure.*　　　　　1 John 3: 2-3

LIFE APPLICATIONS

- Have you ever thought that the Lord Jesus could come before your plans and ambitions have ever materialized?

- Have you ever asked God to direct your path and life's decisions, seeking only to do His will for your life?

- Always put God's love above everything else; walk in love, speak the truth in love and love God in Christ personally by obeying His Word.

DAY 6

The Last Days — Now is the Time!

…it is high time to awake out of sleep; for now our salvation is nearer than when we first believed. The night is far spent, the day is at hand. Therefore let us cast off the works of darkness, and let us put on the armour of light.

Romans 13: 11-12

God never promises tomorrow. Indeed, we do not know what a day will bring forth, so the only acceptable time with God is now!

… Behold, now is the accepted time; behold, now is the day of salvation.　　　　　2 Corinthians 6: 2

The Greek word for time, *kairos,* refers to an appointed time or "season" rather than a certain length of time. The "right time" to receive God's grace is therefore now; that is, when I know He is speaking to me personally! God is always ready to receive me.

When it comes to re-establishing my personal walk with Him, when there are outstanding issues in my life that need to be addressed, when I need to sort myself out with God and get right with Him — when is the right time to do this? The answer is NOW! Tomorrow is never guaranteed, but God is only a step of prayer away whenever we turn to Him! Jesus reassures everyone with His plea —

…the one who comes to Me I will by no means cast out.

John 6: 37

So, I can turn aside, humble myself and ask for forgiveness. I can repent before Him for the things I know are wrong. I can surrender my heart and life to Him, seeking to do His will and not my own.

This list is endless, but God — in Christ — is always there for me, waiting graciously to receive me back if I have wandered astray. His love will NEVER give up on me!

Day 3 showed us —

'Yes, I have loved you with an everlasting love; Therefore with lovingkindness I have drawn you.'

Jeremiah 31:3

God encourages us to seek Him always, to call upon Him, to wait upon Him, to pray to Him, and to cast all our cares upon Him because He cares for us! Yes, Jesus died for us for a reason. Yes, His death was a manifestation of God's love towards each and every person, **but** He also desires our fellowship. His wish is for us to know His love and live with Him forever! Yet, ironically, it has to be repeated: even God cannot make us come to Him or obey Him. We must choose; we must respond to the moving of His love upon our soul through His Spirit as He draws each one to say "yes" to Jesus!

Seek the Lord while He may be found, Call upon Him while he is near. Let the wicked forsake his way, And the unrighteous man his thoughts; Let him return to the Lord, And He will have mercy on him; And to our God, For He will abundantly pardon. Isaiah 55: 6-7

Delay is not wise. Sometimes we can miss God's blessing through lack of response towards Him caused by procrastinating, listening to the lies of the enemy or fear. A good example is in the Old Testament.

God's people, the children of Israel, where in bondage in Egypt, and when their deliverance and the time for Moses to lead them out came, they were commanded to be ready, for they were going to be thrust out of Egypt by the Egyptians. They were even told to sit up all night with their coats on, shoes on their feet and staffs in hand, whilst at the same time eating a good meal of roast lamb, being ready to depart. The bread-dough could not be leavened, for there was not going to be enough time for this lengthy process! Instead, they took the dough with them as it was, unleavened, and they ate unleavened bread in the wilderness as their first meal during their travels. God made an ordinance and the "Feast of Unleavened Bread" to remember this so that they would never forget what happened on that day of His glorious deliverance!

What if some had not obeyed the precise instructions given to them by Moses, deciding perhaps instead to put yeast in the dough and wait for it to prove, a process that takes two to three hours? They would have missed the opportunity to get out of their bondage and slavery, because not too long after the Israelites had left Egypt, Pharaoh changed his mind and decided to bring them back! In this case, there was only one opportunity to obey God. It is not unlike the completely different scenario when a child runs toward the road, not seeing a lorry coming! Instantly, his father shouts for him to stop! Being used to obedience and upon hearing his father's command, the child instantly stops and is saved. Would there have been another opportunity for the child to avoid the lorry had he carried on?

God, however, is gracious. He seeks to teach us the importance of obeying His Word, gently, but firmly. If we fall by the wayside, you can rest assured He will seek to pick us up again. God will never give up on us! In that day in Heaven, we shall truly see that we have only been saved by His grace alone!

One purpose of God's Word, however, is to teach us how to live in this present world (covered extensively in later sessions), and God reminds us that there is coming a day and time when He shall intervene yet once again in human history by returning to this earth — but this time it will be in power and great glory, bringing judgment to the earth in righteousness! Of course, we may have passed away ourselves before that day arrives, but in similitude to the coming of the Lord, none of us knows just when that day will be, so the scenario is very similar. I need to be ready always to meet the Lord!

LIFE APPLICATIONS

- Time will not carry on forever. One day, the world as we know it now will have a visitation; the Lord shall come again and will not tarry. So, whether I am very young and excited with my whole life ahead of me or whether I am old and weary, wishing He would come soon, if I wish to please God, I must always put Him first in everything.

- When did you last hear preached in church the subject of the Lord's Second Coming? When were you last told to be ready to meet the Lord?

DAY 7

The Last Days — As in the Days of Noah

But as the days of Noah were, so also will the coming of the Son of Man be. For as in the days before the flood, they were eating and drinking, marrying and giving in marriage, until the day that Noah entered the ark, and did not know until the flood came and took them all away, so also will the coming of the Son of Man be.   Matthew 24: 37-39

In this final session on the last days, we cannot leave the subject without looking at the intriguing words of Jesus when He likened His coming to the days of Noah prior to when God flooded the earth. In doing so, we see from the above passage that Jesus did not mention the wickedness of those days, even though it is stated in the Bible that the whole earth was covered with corruption and violence! It is probably a good lesson for us not to dwell upon the intricacies of sin and evil, especially when they can be unspeakable, unedifying and utterly despicable.

Even so, commentators of the Bible do believe that verse 2 in Genesis Chapter 6, which says, "*…the sons of God saw the daughters of men, that they were beautiful: and they took wives for themselves of all whom they chose,*" probably refers to angels who rebelliously left Heaven to take women as wives. Though this view has interpretive difficulties, it is probably the most likely; and if this were true, it would only serve to reinforce the pre-flood evil of the world in those days! Whilst "sons of God" could refer to the godly line of Seth, it does not fit that these righteous people would contribute to the exceedingly great wickedness and corruption on the earth that is so greatly emphasized in this passage.

Despite its depraved condition, the Bible does mention godly people on the earth at that time — people such as Enoch, Noah and others. Enoch had this testimony: that he walked with God and pleased God. Even so, at a relatively early age in life, God took him. Could this have been a blessing in disguise to save him from the earth's corruption and destruction in the future?

The earth also was corrupt before God, and the earth was filled with violence. So God looked upon the earth, and indeed it was corrupt; for all flesh had corrupted their way on the earth.   Genesis 6: 11-12

Jesus spoke of the days of Noah in the manner He did for good reason. The fruits of corruption and evil originate from a life of utter indifference to and rejection of the Word of God so that carelessness, selfishness and license become the order of the day. Whenever the Word of God is outrightly rejected by an individual or society at large, it bears a consequence. The enemy of our souls only has room to manoeuvre when we give him the opportunity to do so, and in the last days this will increase more and more, leading to the final intervention of God.

Eating and drinking is perfectly normal; so is marriage and giving in marriage. So why does Jesus refer to these activities in the opening passage when He says —

But as the days of Noah were, so also will the coming of the Son of Man be. For as in the days before the flood, they were eating and drinking, marrying and giving in marriage, until the day that Noah entered the ark, and did not know until the flood came and took them all away…

If I am consumed with a given activity so that it overrides all other responsibilities, then I will eventually be caught out. Jesus addresses the motives of people and their preoccupation with "things" so that what is more important is completely overlooked. I can be told that my train leaves at such and such a time, but unless I prepare in good time beforehand, I can end up missing it! It is possible to be so consumed with other things, which of themselves are not wrong, and completely forget about the train and what I am supposed to be preparing for! God tells us what is happening and that we need to prepare — prepare to meet our God! This is the most important thing in my life, if I did but know it! All else pales into insignificance in comparison, and yet… do I prepare, or do I drift?

When a person rejects God outright, they are on their own but for the hand of God's grace upon them. As pointed out in Genesis, and as suggested in other parts of the Bible, there are seasons and times to come to God. He says:

…"My Spirit shall not strive with man forever…"
Genesis 6:3

Seek the Lord while He may be found, Call upon Him while he is near.
Isaiah 55:6

It behoves those who have been enlightened by God to take heed, lest they fall, by consciously seeking to do His will for their lives each day and not becoming complacent. The above Scriptures serve as a reminder by implying what we may not wish to hear — that there will come a day when God will not always be found!

LIFE APPLICATIONS

- Jesus once said, *"Where your treasure is, there your heart will be also."* What is the most important treasure in my life?

- Noah obeyed God and built the ark according to His instructions, even though he must have appeared to onlookers to be stupid. Am I prepared to put God first in my life irrespective of what others think of me?

PART 2

DAY 8

Living in the Last Days — The World System

It is one thing to be knowledgeable about the last days regarding events that will take place during these times, but how are we to live in them? It is imperative to know what the Bible teaches about how we should live during these latter days — and with God's help we will.

Before we begin, it would be worthwhile to look at how the Bible refers to the fallen world system in which we live. The main source will be the many words of Jesus when he spoke of "the world" as:

1 Under the Rule and influence of Satan;
2 Different and separate from the Kingdom of God.

Then the devil, taking Him up on a high mountain, showed Him all the kingdoms of the world… And the devil said to Him, "All this authority I will give You, and their glory; for this has been delivered to me, and I will give it to whomever I wish. Therefore, if You will worship before me, all will be Yours."   Luke 4: 5-7

Clearly the devil could not give that which he did not have jurisdiction over! It may be a surprise that we are all living in a world under the devil's influence and rule — though looking around us, we may find that not too difficult to comprehend! This is his right, and it's all because man *gave* him his allegiance at The Fall; instead of obeying God, man chose to obey the devil!

Jesus referred to the devil as the "ruler of this world."

*I will no longer talk much with you, for **the ruler of this world** is coming, and he has nothing in Me.*

John 14: 30
(See also John 12:31; 16:11; 1 John 5:19)

Before Pilate, Jesus declared quite openly that His kingdom was not of this world; and on another occasion, He told Jews that He was not of this world's system.

Jesus answered, "My kingdom is not of this world. If My kingdom were of this world, My servants would fight, so that I should not be delivered to the Jews; but now My kingdom is not from here."

John 18: 36
(See also John 8: 23)

The word "world" — Greek *kosmos* — means "orderly arrangement and beauty," but now the biblical word for "world" tends to focus upon "the earth" as the secular world contrasted with Heaven. In fact, this word in the New Testament describes a world system alienated from and opposed to God and, as already mentioned, a system that is in the power of the Evil One.

Our position, therefore, as children of God is that we are in the world but not of the world, having been born again into God's Kingdom! This was included in the Jesus' prayer to His Father prior to His going to the cross. The words of Jesus are so revealing in this passage, regarding our current subject, that it is worth reading the whole chapter at this point!

Jesus spoke these words, lifted up His eyes to heaven, and said: "Father, the hour has come. Glorify Your Son, that Your Son also may glorify You, as You have given Him authority over all flesh, that He should give eternal life to as many as You have given Him. And this is eternal life, that they may know You, the only true God, and Jesus Christ whom You have sent. I have glorified You on the earth. I have finished the work which You have given Me to do. And now, **O Father, glorify Me together with Yourself, with the Glory which I had with You before the world was.**

"I have manifested Your name to the men whom You have given Me out of the world. They were Yours, You gave them to Me, and they have kept Your word. Now they have known that all things which You have given Me are from You. For I have given to them the words which You have given Me; and they have received them, and have known surely **that I came forth from You; and they have believed that You sent Me.**

"I pray for them. I do not pray for the world but for those whom You have given Me, for they are Yours. And all Mine are Yours, and Yours are Mine, and I am glorified in them. Now I am no longer in the world, but these are in the world, and I come to You. Holy Father, keep through Your name those whom You have given Me, that they may be one as We are. While I was with them in the world, I kept them in Your name. Those whom You gave Me I have kept; and none of them is lost except the son of perdition, that the Scripture might be fulfilled.

"But now I come to You, and these things I speak in the world, that they may have My joy fulfilled in themselves. I have given them Your word; and the world has hated them because **they are not of the world, just as I am not of the world.** *I do not pray that You should take them out of the world, but that You should keep them from the evil one.* **They are not of the world, just as I am not of the world.** *Sanctify them by Your truth. Your word is truth. As You sent Me into the world, I also have sent them into the world. And for their sakes I sanctify Myself, that they also may be sanctified by the truth.*

"I do not pray for these alone, but also for those who will believe in Me through their word; that they all may be one, as You, Father, are in Me, and I in You; that they also may be one in Us, that the world may believe that You sent Me. And the glory which You gave Me I have given them, that they may be one just as We are one: I in them, and You in Me; that they may be made perfect in one, and that the world may know that You have sent Me, and have loved them as You have loved Me.

"Father, I desire that they also whom You gave Me may be with Me where I am, that they may behold My glory which You have given Me; for You loved Me before the foundation of the world.

"O righteous Father! The world has not known You, but I have known You; and these have known that You sent Me. And I have declared to them Your name, and will declare it, that the love with which You loved Me may be in them, and I in them."

John 17

As we read this chapter, said by some to be the real "Lord's prayer," we see the living reality of the relationship between the Father and the Son and understand much more about "the world" from the point of view of Jesus Himself — in contrast to the home of His father!

Do not love the world or the things in the world. If anyone loves the world, the love of the Father is not in him. For all that is in the world…. is not of the Father but is of the world.

1 John 2: 15-16

This passage of Scripture is to be understood in the light of what is meant by "the world" as a system that is anti-God.

We are to understand this biblical perspective so as to clearly perceive the real situation. It is by no means a recipe to avoid our responsibilities towards seeking to maintain and keep the earth, recognizing the original beauty and God's order that He created. Neither is it an excuse to avoid our responsibilities in this life: working with our hands that which is good, fulfilling God's original intention for us—which has not changed! It is, however, to understand and realise that the "world" and the "Kingdom of God" are two very different and distinct places. One is ruled by the Evil One and the other by God! We are to decide where our allegiance lies. Jesus said that His followers were *in* the world but not *of* it!

LIFE APPLICATIONS

- How has this biblical perspective of "the world" affected your thinking?

- The "Lord's Prayer" as recorded in John 17, and the way Jesus spoke about this world, His Kingdom and all those who would be saved, provides a blueprint of essential facts about this present world and the one to come. It presents a profound and sound basis for our faith in Jesus, seeing that it is He Who speaks!

DAY 9

Living in the Last Days — The World's Temptations

To understand this, it is better to go right back to the beginning when man was first tempted into sin by choosing to adhere to and obey the words of Satan and not the words spoken by God.

The Temptation and Fall of Man

Now the serpent was more cunning than any beast of the field which the Lord God had made. And he said to the woman, "Has God indeed said, 'You shall not eat of every tree of the garden'?"

And the woman said to the serpent, "We may eat the fruit of the trees of the garden; but of the fruit of the tree which is in the midst of the garden, God has said, 'You shall not eat it, nor shall you touch it, lest you die.'"

Then the serpent said to the woman, "You will not surely die For God knows that in the day you eat of it your eyes will be opened, and you will be like God, knowing good and evil."

So when the woman saw that the tree was good for food, that it was pleasant to the eyes, and a tree desirable to make one wise, she took of its fruit and ate. She also gave to her husband with her, and he ate.   Genesis 3: 1-6

The above passage outlines what the Bible says about the original temptation of man, where the word "man" is used to represent mankind. By examining this, we can learn much about the elements that comprise temptation.

Firstly, we see that *the serpent* – identified in Revelation 12: 9 as Satan himself – is cunning, crafty and shrewd.

*"Has God indeed said, 'You shall not eat of **every** tree of the garden'?"*

In other words, he was saying, 'All this is not enough; you are missing out! You could have more!'

In life we can, at some time, feel a sense of lack, perhaps wishing for things to be different, being dissatisfied by our situation, our appearance or simply by the lot life has thrown us! How many people believe that if they could only perhaps win the lottery or have a lot more material wealth it would be the answer to all their hopes and dreams, even though we are told that many such millionaires simply squander their sudden material gain away and end up all the worse for it?

Jesus said:

… "Take heed, and beware of covetousness, for one's life does not consist in the abundance of the things he possesses."   Luke 12:15

As much as we all need money, it is not in itself the answer to life. An Ace card the devil plays is to make us feel inadequate just as we are and to convince us that we need more.

God was blessing Adam, speaking to him positively by saying:

… "Of every tree of the garden, you may freely eat; but of the tree of the knowledge of good and evil you shall not eat, for in the day that you eat of it you shall surely die."   Genesis 2:16-17

God, in all His generosity, added only one proviso, but despite that Satan was seeking to instil a sense of lack by speaking negatively.

*"Has God indeed said, 'You shall not eat of **every** tree of the garden'?"*

And it worked!

Beware! Satan always twists God's Word. Remember Jesus, when He was being tempted Himself in the wilderness? Satan was misquoting God's Word, attempting to persuade Jesus to yield His allegiance to him — but it did not work!

Back in the garden, Satan went further and lied to Eve.

Then the serpent said to the woman, "You will not surely die For God knows that in the day you eat of it your eyes will be opened, and you will be like God, knowing good and evil."

Temptation and deception are achieved when we submit to something we consider to be seemingly better outwardly and greater than what is on offer. However, it is merely appeasing to a personal inward desire to satisfy our selfishness, worldly ambitions and desires, called in the Bible, "the lust of the flesh, the lust of the eyes and the pride of life."

We can always rest assured that if it is against God's Word then we do well to dismiss it and submit ourselves to God Who is able to save us from temptation.

No temptation has overtaken you except such as is common to man; but God is faithful, who will not allow you to be tempted beyond what you are able, but with the temptation will also make the way of escape, that you may be able to bear it.   1 Corinthians 10:13

Finally, Eve succumbed to the temptation to defy the Words of God and chose to give her allegiance to the words of Satan.

So when the woman saw that the tree was good for food [the lust of the flesh], *that it was pleasant to the eyes* [the lust of the eyes], *and a tree desirable to make one wise* [the pride of life], *she took of its fruit and ate. She also gave to her husband with her, and he ate.*

The aim of the devil is to make you believe his ways give you much more pleasure, that the present, temporary attractions of outward appearance cannot be discarded, and that the wisdom and knowledge of his world is a superior way to the order of God's Word.

This is a lie! God's Word says true life, joy and fulfilment are only found in our Creator!

… In Your presence is fullness of joy; At Your right hand are pleasures forevermore.   Psalm 16:11

… "Eye has not seen, nor ear heard, Nor have entered into the heart of man the things which God has prepared for those who love Him."   1 Corinthians 2:9

God's joy comes as a result of living in truth, righteousness and holiness. God is essentially unselfish and humble. The joy of God's salvation, through Jesus Christ in sacrificing Himself for sinful man and thereby bringing many souls into His Kingdom, is unspeakable and full of glory! The crescendo of worship in Heaven will one day resonate throughout all eternity, and the Lamb will be forever seen, recognised and remembered for what He has achieved. He will bear the nail prints upon His hands — the eternal evidence of our salvation in and through Him! Can you imagine the response as Jesus lifts up His hands in praise, His scars being lit up with the glory of God?

❖ Jesus, through His victorious work on the cross, has destroyed **all the works of devil**:

   …For this purpose, the Son of God was manifested, that He might destroy the works of the devil.
   1 John 3:8

❖ Jesus has provided a way for us to be forgiven through repentance and turning to God.

❖ Forgetting the past, God lovingly receives us through Christ as sons and daughters!

   Behold what manner of love the Father has bestowed on us, that we should be called children of God!
   1 John 3:1

❖ Jesus has reassured us by giving us His promise.

*"Most assuredly, I say to you, he who hears My word and believes in Him who sent Me has everlasting life, and shall **not come into judgment**, but has passed from death into life.*
John 5: 24

LIFE APPLICATIONS

- Adam and Eve were given everything they needed by God, but they were beguiled into a sense of lack and feeling dissatisfied! Are you dissatisfied with life at this present moment?

- Only by trusting God's Word to direct us throughout our life can we escape Satan's power over us through our sinful human nature.

- Believe that God's Word is always for you and never against you!

DAY 10

Living in the Last Days —
How We Should Live: Denying Worldly Lusts

*For the grace of God that brings salvation has appeared to all men, teaching us that, **denying** ungodliness and **worldly lusts**, we should live soberly, righteously, and godly in the present age, looking for the blessed hope and glorious appearing of our great God and Saviour Jesus Christ.*

Titus 2:11-13

This Scripture presents a concise description of how the child of God should **live** in this world during the last days and gives specific instruction to every believer. For this reason, we shall focus upon it to identify what exactly is being said and examine all that it entails in practice!

It is this life-application approach to the Bible that is vital if we are to live the way God prescribes. It is one thing to believe the Scriptures and another to receive and apply their truths to your own personal life. As a Christian, your life in the future will be determined by your choices. Therefore, the children of God should begin by dedicating their lives to the Lord, making it their goal always to seek to please the One who loves them and has died for them!

We see in the above passage, that you cannot begin to live the way God desires until you have yourself *denied ungodliness and worldly lusts*. This is basically part of the process of repentance, turning away from sin and looking to God thereafter. It's like receiving God's free gift of eternal life; you cannot live the new life God has for you without turning away from the old life first. You

46

cannot put new wine into old bottles!

What are worldly lusts?

First, it is necessary to examine the word "lust" and see what this means in the Bible. The root meaning of this word has the same root meaning as "desire" and can be interpreted as follows:

- To set one's heart upon
- Eagerly long for
- Covet greatly

The word emphasizes the intensity of the desire rather than the object being desired. By this definition, it can therefore be used to describe both good and evil desires.

Three times in the New Testament it is applied to good desires:

*Then He said to them, "With fervent **desire** I have **desired** to eat this Passover with you before I suffer;"*
Luke 22:15

*"For I am hard-pressed between the two, having a **desire** to depart and be with Christ, which is far better."*
Philippians 1:23

*"But we, brethren, having been taken away from you for a short time in presence, not in heart, endeavoured more eagerly to see your face with great **desire**."*
1 Thessalonians 2:17

Its other uses are negative and the word "lust" is used to describe:

- Gratifying sensual cravings
- Desiring the forbidden
- Coveting what belongs to someone else
- Striving for things, persons or experiences contrary to the will of God

Paul's instruction to young Timothy was to:

> *Flee also youthful **lusts**, but pursue righteousness, faith, love, peace with those who call on the Lord out of a pure heart.*
> 2 Timothy 2:22

Whenever the word "lust" is used, therefore, in the Scriptures, it represents the evil form of "intense desires." Hence, we are to live in this present age *"denying ungodliness and **worldly lusts.**"* Reference to the study on Day 8 will provide clear understanding of what is meant by "worldly" lusts.

Satan's control in and through the sinful human nature of unregenerate man enables him to exert his evil influence. This sphere of evil operating in our world has therefore contaminated people throughout every part of the world's systems. We are continually warned and reminded about this in the Scriptures:

> *For all that is in the world — the **lust** of the flesh, the **lust** of the eyes, and the pride of life — is not of the Father but is of the world. And the world is passing away, and the **lust** of it; but he who does the will of God abides forever.*
> 1 John 2:16-17

The world, as we know it, is temporary! We are in the world, but the world is not our home. "I'm just a passin' through,"[iii] sang a famous singer! Sometimes, the Bible refers to this by describing God's children as sojourners and pilgrims on the earth.

> *Beloved, I beg you as sojourners and pilgrims, abstain from fleshly **lusts** which war against the soul.*
>
> 1 Peter 2:11

Read also the passage in Hebrews 11: 13-16.

> *These all died in faith, not having received the promises, but having seen them afar off were assured of them, embraced them and confessed that they were **strangers and pilgrims on the earth.** For those who say such things declare plainly that they seek a homeland. And truly if they had called to mind that country from which they had come out, they would have had opportunity to return. But now they desire a better, that is, a heavenly country. Therefore God is not ashamed to be called their God, for He has prepared a city for them.*

The Bible says that wrong desires are the cause of strife and all wars!

> *Where do wars and fights come from among you? Do they not come from your **desires** for pleasure that war in your members? You **lust** and do not have. You murder and covet and cannot obtain…*
>
> James 4:1-2

We can have new desires when the Holy Spirit comes to dwell in us. He imparts the things of God and reveals Jesus to us. The Psalmist, David, knew this only too well. Having failed in the area of lust, he had through repentance turned back to God.

A favourite Psalm of mine is Psalm 27, part of which is below:

> *The Lord is my light and my salvation;*
> *Whom shall I fear?*
> *The Lord is the strength of my life;*
> *Of whom shall I be afraid?*
> *When the wicked came against me*
> *To eat up my flesh,*
> *My enemies and foes,*
> *They stumbled and fell.*
> *Though an army may encamp against me,*
> *My heart shall not fear;*
> *Though war may rise against me,*
> *In this I will be confident.*
> ***One thing I have desired of the Lord,***
> *That will I seek:*
> *That I may dwell in the house of the Lord*
> *All the days of my life,*
> *To behold the beauty of the Lord,*
> *And to inquire in His temple.*

LIFE APPLICATIONS

- Recognize that temptations to lust after things are all part of our fallen nature called "the flesh" and that we must continually turn to Christ and God's Word. By the power of the Holy Spirit within us, God is able to keep us.

"…He who is in you is greater than he who is in the world." 1 John 4:4

- Recognize that in this present world we are in a battle of good against evil. But remember: whilst there will be many battles, in Jesus we will always have the victory!

Jesus said in John 16:33,

"... In the world you will have tribulation; but be of good cheer, I have overcome the world."

DAY 11

Living in the Last Days — Living Soberly

*For the grace of God that brings salvation has appeared to all men, teaching us that, denying ungodliness and worldly lusts, we should **live soberly**, righteously, and godly in the present age, looking for the blessed hope and glorious appearing of our great God and Saviour Jesus Christ.*

Titus 2:11-13

We shall first look at what is meant by the word "soberly" in this text. In doing so, we must understand right from the outset that it is only by the grace of God that we can achieve what is required by God — and by no other means! There is not a recipe or list of rules and instructions leading us to our own self-righteousness, but there is a work of grace in our lives as we submit to God! Whatever God requires, it will be doable by a willing heart.

Ephesians 2:8-9 tells us our salvation is by grace alone:

For by grace you have been saved through faith, and that not of yourselves; it is the gift of God, not of works, lest anyone should boast.

Similarly, here in Titus 2:11-12, we read that we are to be taught by His grace.

***For the grace of God** that brings salvation has appeared to all men, teaching us that... we should **live soberly**...*

The word "soberly" describes what our attitude and behaviour should be as we approach the ending of the age. It means:

- acting in a responsible manner, sensibly, prudently;
- being in self-control;
- being in full possession of intellectual and emotional faculties; or
- of right mind.

A relevant passage to compare is found in Mark 5:15 and will give us greater enlightenment. This passage in the context of a demon-possessed man who Jesus healed.

*Then they came to Jesus, and saw the one who had been demon-possessed and had the legion, sitting and clothed and in his **right mind**. And they were afraid.*

This verse describes the transformation of the demon-possessed man who now behaved quite differently than before. He was now in his "right mind." This description is similar in meaning to the word "sober."

The Greek word for "soberly" is *sophronos* and for "right mind" is *sophroneo*. In other words, to live soberly in this present age may be described as living with a right mind or being of sound mind! The onlookers to this miracle performed by Jesus in Mark 5 were afraid, for they knew that the man had been possessed of an unclean spirit, but now they saw him acting in a sensible, responsible manner, being in full possession of his faculties. Compare this description with the above meaning of the word "sober."

I am immediately reminded of that special verse of Scripture that talks of having a sound mind —

*For God has not given us a spirit of fear, but of power and of love and of a **sound mind.*** 2 Timothy 1:7

So, by God's grace and with the empowering of the Holy Spirit within us, we can begin to learn how to live in these last days the way God wants us to live — being sober and of a sound mind.

We only need to look at the opposites to living soberly or consider the antithesis of having a sound mind to realize that man's ways are not God's ways! Instead of "self-control," there is no control whatsoever; instead of "acting in a responsible or sensible manner" — which is sometimes frowned upon — there is an increasing desire to do as one pleases without any restraint.

Below are some examples taken from the Bible of how the world system has been controlled by Satan, influencing mankind through the lusts of his sinful human nature.

Now the works of the flesh are evident, which are: adultery, fornication, uncleanness, lewdness, idolatry, sorcery, hatred, contentions, jealousies, outbursts of wrath, selfish ambitions, dissensions, heresies, envy, murders, drunkenness, revelries, and the like; of which I tell you beforehand, just as I also told you in time past, that those who practice such things will not inherit the kingdom of God.
Galatians 5:19-21

And all these are in stark contrast to the ways of God's Kingdom:

But the fruit of the Spirit is love, joy, peace, longsuffering, kindness, goodness, faithfulness, gentleness, self-control. Against such there is no law.

Galatians 5:22-23

We do not have a sound mind until we have the mind of Christ; we are never free from fear until we have God's perfect love that casts out all fear!

Thank God who gives us the victory through our Lord Jesus Christ!

LIFE APPLICATIONS

- Given the stark contrast between the Kingdom of God and the Kingdom of this world, which Kingdom are you most loyal to?

- In your walk with God, can you truly say that you are not walking with fear but with God's power, love and a sound mind as presented in 2 Timothy 1:7?

- Ask: Am I willing to wholly give myself to becoming a disciple of Jesus Christ by allowing His grace to teach me how I should live in this present age?

THOUGHT

But the end of all things is at hand; therefore be serious and watchful in your prayers. And above all things have fervent love for one another, for "love will cover a multitude of sins."

1 Peter 4:7

DAY 12

Living in the Last Days —
Living Righteously: What Does This Mean?

*For the grace of God that brings salvation has appeared to all men, teaching us that, denying ungodliness and worldly lusts, we should live soberly, **righteously**, and godly in the present age, looking for the blessed hope and glorious appearing of our great God and Saviour Jesus Christ.*

Titus 2:11-13

What does it mean to live **righteously** in the present age? And indeed, how does one become righteous in the first place? Let's face it; the whole prospect of living a righteous life may sound daunting to some: "After all, I don't particularly feel righteous, because I still make so many mistakes."

The Word of God will show us without any shadow of a doubt that it is a condition for us to be righteous and to live righteously in this present age. Therefore, we need to look at what is expected of the child of God, the born-again believer, according to the Scriptures.

First, we shall consider what makes a person righteous — or put differently, being right with God.

The Bible declares quite emphatically that righteousness is not attained by our own good works, but it is attributed to those who believe what God says about Jesus and the finished work of the cross!

*For He made Him who knew no sin to be sin for us, that we might become **the righteousness of God** in Him.*

2 Corinthians 5:21

This verse tells us that Jesus bore our sins on the cross and endured the penalty that we deserved **that we might become the righteousness of God in Him!** So, God saves sinners and attributes to them righteousness as they believe in Christ who died in their stead — the just for the unjust.

Romans 3:21-24 gives further clarification and understanding.

*But now **the righteousness of God** apart from the law is revealed, being witnessed by the Law and the Prophets, **even the righteousness of God, through faith in Jesus Christ,** to all and on all who believe. For there is no difference; for all have sinned and fall short of the glory of God, being **justified** freely by His **grace**…*

The word "justified" is a legal word and means, "to acquit and declare righteous." God's righteousness was never intended to be attained by keeping the Law but by faith in Him. The Law declared man as a sinner, for he could not keep it, and therefore God was teaching and preparing His people to understand that they could only be made right with Him through His mercy and forgiveness. This was thus pointing the way to the atoning work of the Blood of the Lamb, which became fulfilled in His Son, Jesus Christ, on the cross.

No person can be justified by their own good works, for the standard is beyond man's reach! The following Scripture makes this very clear:

[K]nowing that a man is not justified by the works of the law but by faith in Jesus Christ, even we have believed in Christ Jesus, that we might be justified by faith in Christ and

not by the works of the law; for by the works of the law no flesh shall be justified.

Galatians 2:16

Sadly, many "good" people in the world consider themselves above reproach and acceptable to God, having lived a good and moral life. But it is their hardness of heart, arrogance and self-righteousness that, if unrepented of, will bar them entry into God's Kingdom. The Bible is clear:

[F]or all have sinned and fall short of the glory of God.

Romans 3:23

The Lord looks down from heaven upon the children of men, To see if there are any who understand, who seek God. They have all turned aside, They have together become corrupt; **There is none who does good, No, not one.**

Psalm 14:2-3

(See also Romans 3:10-12)

Paul the Apostle was an educated, religious man who, at the first, trusted in his own righteousness, being a scholar of the Law and having been taught at the feet of Gamaliel, a highly recognised teacher of the Jewish law and a Pharisee. Paul acquired expert knowledge of the Hebrew Scriptures, but having found Christ, he had this to say:

But what things were gain to me, these I have counted loss for Christ. Yet indeed I also count all things loss for the excellence of the knowledge of Christ Jesus my Lord, for whom I have suffered the loss of all things, and count them as rubbish, that I may gain Christ and be found in Him, not having my own righteousness, which is from the law, but that which is through faith in Christ, the righteousness which is from God by faith.   Philippians 3:7-9

LIFE APPLICATIONS

- The message is very clear: to be right with God we must accept God's free gift in Jesus. It is the only way we can be accepted as righteous before God.

  … for there is no other name under Heaven given among men by which we must be saved.   Acts 4:12

- Is there a specific time in your life when you, as a church-goer or one who professes to be a Christian, did this for yourself—accepted Jesus Christ as your Lord and Saviour?

DAY 13

Living in the Last Days —
Living Righteously: Submitting to God

*For the grace of God that brings salvation has appeared to all men, teaching us that, denying ungodliness and worldly lusts, we should live soberly, **righteously**, and godly in the present age, looking for the blessed hope and glorious appearing of our great God and Saviour Jesus Christ.*

Titus 2:11-13

A well-known saying in Christian circles is, "I am saved, I am being saved, and I shall be saved!"

A person is saved only by God's grace through faith in Christ, and it is true to say at conversion that "**I am saved**." This is when I become a born-again Christian and a child of God, having received Jesus as my Lord and Saviour.

At the end of my life in Christ or when Jesus returns, it is also true to say that I shall then **be saved** to live with and forever be with the Lord! The Bible calls it the redemption of our body.

*...even we ourselves groan within ourselves, eagerly waiting for the adoption, **the redemption of our body**. For we were saved in this hope...* Romans 8:23-24

As we live on this earth, we shall need to confess our sins before the Lord constantly as He works in our lives, teaching and correcting us, and therefore it is true to say that, in this respect, we are **being saved**.

If we say that we have no sin, we deceive ourselves, and the truth is not in us. If we confess our sins, He is faithful and just to forgive us our sins and to cleanse us from all unrighteousness.   1 John 1:8-9

It is this **right living** with God that is paramount if we are to understand the requirement of God's Word to live **righteously** in the present age. You see, when put simply, I can never make myself righteous before God, as already seen on Day 12. It is impossible and unattainable. So God, having accepted the righteousness of Christ and His atoning blood for my sin, receives me in Him and works in my life a process called sanctification and cleansing. The Bible calls this, in one place, learning to walk according to the Spirit.

There is therefore now no condemnation to those who are in Christ Jesus, who do not walk according to the flesh, but according to the Spirit.   Romans 8:1

Righteous living, whilst a commandment, is nevertheless subject to my will. I must choose to **submit** myself to Him and allow Him to work in me and make me more like Christ. It is this submissive attitude of heart to the Lord that today's reading focuses upon.

*I beseech you therefore, brethren, by the mercies of God, that **you present your bodies** a living sacrifice, holy, acceptable to God, which is your reasonable service. And do not be conformed to this world, but be transformed by the renewing of your mind, that you may prove what is that good and acceptable and perfect will of God.*   Romans 12:1-2

This passage of Scripture forms a sound basis for our Christian walk with God and tells us of **our** requirement to **submit** ourselves to Him that our minds may be transformed from the inherited worldly way of thinking — that is, thinking according to our human nature — to the mind of Christ.

We are called to be changed into the image of Christ from glory to glory, to live out Christ and reflect Him before people. That is why it is necessary for each person to follow through on this commitment to God of their own free will and partner up with Him.

One might then ask, "Why has God saved me?"

Of course, God desires to save each one, because He loves us and has demonstrated this fact by sending His Son to die on the cross for us. However, the Bible teaches that God desires us to be *conformed to the image of His Son;* in other words, we are to be like Him! (Romans 8:29)

This is a life-long process, and as mentioned, it requires our cooperation and willingness to **submit** to Him. Our real identity and purpose in life will then begin to unfold!

Only through God's Word can the Holy Spirit teach us about Christ as He speaks to our inner heart.

You will never be alone. Jesus has promised never to leave you, nor forsake you. Choose today to enter God's pathway rather than your own, fulfilling His purposes for your life and doing the works He has determined and planned for you. In doing so, you will be accomplishing something impossible to do by yourself — learning to live **righteously** in the present age, step by step and from glory unto glory!

Therefore He is also able to save to the uttermost those who come to God through Him, since He always lives to make intercession for them.   Hebrews 7:25

LIFE APPLICATIONS

- Did I make Jesus both Lord and Saviour of my life at conversion?

- Did I give my life to God when He saved me, desiring His plans and purposes for my life?

- Am I willing to let God take over the reins of my life so that I will always obey Him in every choice and decision I make?

A PRAYER

Father, thank you for sending Your Son into this world to save me and forgive all my sin.
Forgive me for ever holding back on You, choosing to follow my own ways and not relying upon Your guidance for my life.
Lord, I choose this day to give my life afresh to You.
I ask You to teach me, help and guide me.
I submit myself to You, choosing to read Your Word and spend time with You each day in prayer.
Amen.

DAY 14

Living in the Last Days — Living Righteously:
The Righteousness Which Is of God

*For the grace of God that brings salvation has appeared to all men, teaching us that, denying ungodliness and worldly lusts, we should live soberly, **righteously**, and godly in the present age, looking for the blessed hope and glorious appearing of our great God and Saviour Jesus Christ.*

Titus 2:11-13

*For He made Him who knew no sin to be sin for us, that we might become **the righteousness of God** in Him.*

2 Corinthians 5:21

On Day 12 we looked at how, through faith in Christ and by believing and yielding our lives to Him, we are **declared righteous** in Him! This is a biblical truth in the same way that we are also declared, in Christ, to be **chosen, holy, blameless, adopted, accepted, redeemed, and forgiven**. The essence of this is found in full below:

*Blessed be the God and Father of our Lord Jesus Christ, who has blessed us with every spiritual blessing in the heavenly places in Christ, just as **He chose us** in Him before the foundation of the world, that we should be **holy and without blame** before Him in love, having predestined us to **adoption** as sons by Jesus Christ to Himself, according to the good pleasure of His will, to the praise of the glory of His grace, by which He made us **accepted** in the Beloved.*

*In Him we have **redemption** through His blood, the **forgiveness** of sins, according to the riches of His grace.*

Ephesians 1:3-7

On Day 13 we read about how we must submit ourselves to and partner with God on a day-to-day basis so that the Holy Spirit can teach us to walk righteously transforming us into the image of Christ. As we saw, this is not a technical process but one that operates by God's personal love and grace to each one—Christ in me the hope of glory! My attributed or imputed righteousness is all by God's grace; I utterly depend upon Jesus every step of the way, right up until I enter Heaven's gates to see Him—without fear.

Think about this! There is no condemnation in Christ Jesus! I am free to love God and serve Him! He abides in me in the person of the Holy Spirit to guide, comfort and teach me—and to chastise and correct me when necessary! Jesus died for me, because He loves me and desires this personal relationship with me.

Paul the Apostle was confident of this, having yielded himself to God on the Damascus road. He had previously been an enemy of Christians, arranging for them to be chained and killed. After his encounter with Christ and hearing and seeing for himself, he believed on Him, repented of all his past life and gave himself to Jesus as a servant forever! Once a person truly sees Who Jesus is, this could be their response. Consequently, Paul could say:

*For I am already being poured out as a drink offering, and the time of my departure is at hand. I have fought the good fight, I have finished the race, I have kept the faith. Finally, there is laid up for me the **crown of righteousness**, which the Lord, the righteous Judge, **will give to me** on that Day, and not to me only but also to all who have loved His appearing.*

2 Timothy 4:6-8

Where did Paul's confidence originate? Did it come because of all the good works he had done? No! Rather, it came by faith in the Lord and his understanding of all that Jesus had acquired for him by His grace! In his declaration, he also gave others the same assurance when he said, "and not to me only but also to all who have loved His appearing." Paul knew that the whole prospect of Heaven and reward was based upon God's grace alone.

This is understanding the righteousness of God in Christ! This is being illuminated and seeing the realm that God now works in—not by my works, but by His grace alone!

LIFE APPLICATIONS

- What was your own understanding of Christ's victory on the cross and all that it has achieved for every believer?

- Has reading this day's meditations increased your knowledge and enlightened you in any way?

- The calling of God is specific and different for every believer in that God has chosen each person to do good works that only he/she can accomplish!

- Can you, like Paul the Apostle, say that, having believed in Jesus, you have surrendered your life to Him to be His servant forever?

DAY 15

Living in the Last Days — A Godly Life:
Following On To Know the Lord

*For the grace of God that brings salvation has appeared to all men, teaching us that, denying ungodliness and worldly lusts, we should live soberly, righteously, and **godly** in the present age, looking for the blessed hope and glorious appearing of our great God and Saviour Jesus Christ.*

Titus 2:11-13

As we look at the wonderful declarations of grace and salvation we have received through Christ, it is good to pause and consider just how these attributes work out in practice.

On Day 14 we saw these amazing blessings of God the Father declared in Ephesians Chapter 1:

*Blessed be the God and Father of our Lord Jesus Christ, who has blessed us with every spiritual blessing in the heavenly places in Christ, **just as He chose us in Him before the foundation of the world, that we should be holy and without blame before Him in love, having predestined us to adoption as sons by Jesus Christ to Himself, according to the good pleasure of His will, to the praise of the glory of His grace, by which He made us accepted in the Beloved.***

In Him we have redemption through His blood, *the forgiveness of sins...*

Ephesians 1:3-7

This wonderful picture of God's love is revealed in the parable of the prodigal son. The whole basis of this story is the presentation of what God has prepared for those who turn to Him in repentance.

This revelation began when the wayward son came to himself and said:

… 'How many of my father's hired servants have bread enough and to spare, and I perish with hunger! I will arise and go to my father, and will say to him, "Father, I have sinned against heaven and before you, and I am no longer worthy to be called your son. Make me like one of your hired servants."' And he arose and came to his father…　　Luke 15:17-20

Here is an important truth. The work of the cross — when Jesus paid the price for our sins — has opened the door of grace to the Father. God is now in position to save all those who come to Him through Jesus, just as when the prodigal son chose to repent and turn aside from the wayward living that had led him to ruin, he found that his father was already waiting and looking out for him!

This is what grace is! It is God's lovingkindness towards us, through no work or merit of our own; and, as mentioned, has its very roots in the death of Jesus, His Son.

Obeying laws could never make us perfect. God has chosen a different way — the way of grace and forgiveness that came at a very high price, the blood of Jesus.

Upon returning to his father, the prodigal son received the blessings and had learned his lesson, choosing now to follow a different pathway — living in his father's household. This is the picture: having received all the benefits of a loving God, we now follow on to know the Lord!

"Living a Godly Life," the title of today's meditation, is God's way of working change within us.

Because of the nature of God's salvation, it is very clear what He requires from each one — a heart response by giving Him our heart! Practically, it involves yielding to Him that my life be changed from glory unto glory. The Bible says that our lives are not our own; we have been bought with a price, and it is needful for each child of God to recognise this fact and give themselves wholeheartedly to God and His will for their lives.

This is God's way! This is the way Jesus came into the world, not desiring to do His own will but the will of the Father Who sent Him. Jesus is the way, the truth and the life; no one comes to the Father but by Him.

The days we are living in are perilous times — the end times — and we, as God's children, must sharpen our swords by reading more of God's Word and allowing the Holy Spirit to work change in us. Jesus said:

"They are not of the world, just as I am not of the world. Sanctify them by Your truth. Your word is truth."
John 17:16-17

As we read God's Word, it is the work of the Holy Spirit to help us renew our minds to the things of God's Kingdom—to the things belonging to Christ—thus making us more like Him. This is God's will for you!

In addition, we cannot be forgiven in isolation; we need to learn how to forgive like the Father.

If we are without blame before God, then we need to learn how not to blame others.

If we are made acceptable in Him through Christ, we need to learn how to love and accept others through the eyes of Christ.

If God looks upon us without sin in Christ, we need to submit our members to God and learn how not to sin habitually.

If God looks upon us as being holy in Christ, we need to learn how to walk in holiness.

LIFE APPLICATIONS

- Although God desires the salvation of all, He does not violate our opportunity to choose. Will you yield your life to Him today with a heart willing to obey and do His will?

- Since God does not compel me to obey Him but allows me to choose, it is necessary I respond to His grace for myself.

  See, I have set before you today life and good, death and evil… therefore choose life…   Deuteronomy 30:15-19

- God's love has greater demands upon me than the law ever could, and since He has demonstrated His love towards me by sending His Son to die upon a cross, it behoves me to come to Him while He is near.

  [H]ow shall we escape if we neglect so great a salvation?
  Hebrews 2:3

DAY 16

Living in the Last Days —
A Godly Life: Facing Conflicts

*For the grace of God that brings salvation has appeared to all men, teaching us that, denying ungodliness and worldly lusts, we should live soberly, righteously, and **godly** in the present age, looking for the blessed hope and glorious appearing of our great God and Saviour Jesus Christ.*

Titus 2:11-13

According to 2 Timothy 3:1-5, perilous times will come in the last days. It is relevant in today's meditation to look at this passage:

*But know this, that in the last days perilous times will come: For men will be lovers of themselves, lovers of money, boasters, proud, blasphemers, disobedient to parents, unthankful, unholy, unloving, unforgiving, slanderers, without self-control, brutal, despisers of good, traitors, headstrong, haughty, lovers of pleasure rather than lovers of God, **having a form of godliness but denying its power...**

In the last days, people will be characterized by all kinds of self-centred and unnatural perversions. Some will maintain an outward pretence, probably speaking the vocabulary of Christianity but rejecting the reality that Christian faith expresses.

The **power** they deny is the heart of Christianity — the fact of a risen Saviour; the truth of the inspired Word of God; and the indwelling and overflowing of the Holy Spirit, working within believers and transforming their lives. Whatever this "form of godliness" is, we are told to turn away from it.

Let us not be deceived; already, increasing numbers denounce Christ and all He stands for, seeking to compromise long-standing beliefs in the Holy Scriptures to accommodate the world's views and so-called "modern thinking." Through their assertion and demand for "human rights" and "equality," many are dissatisfied with current legislation, aggressively seeking to legitimise their beliefs and practices by making them law. It is a matter of controversy that the things being demanded are usually contrary to biblical truths.

Ardent followers of Christ who desire to adhere to the written Word of God are being marginalised and considered to be out of touch with modern-day thinking. They can be considered as extreme or referred to as fundamentalist in a derogatory manner, ridiculed and ostracized, thus increasingly ushering in those perilous times previously spoken of and declared in the Bible long ago as prophetic signs that are now coming to pass before our very eyes!

God's Word declares itself to be the same yesterday, today and forever, and that it will endure forever. Jesus said, "Heaven and earth will pass away, but My words will by no means pass away." (Matthew 24:35)

How futile it is, therefore, to seek to change and denounce the eternal Word of God by which all the world will be judged! In attempting to do so, sinful man will be unconsciously or otherwise working in conjunction with the very plans and purposes of Satan himself, setting themselves in direct conflict with God.

Consequently, there will be opposition towards those who believe the true Gospel. Jesus Himself said:

> *"These things I have spoken to you, that in Me you may have peace. In the world you will have tribulation; but be of good cheer, I have overcome the world."*   John 16:33

Living a Godly life is living like He has told us to live; this involves studying and applying the Scriptures. Those who do so will become a living reproof to those who do not, and thus they will often encounter persecution. But though darkness covers the entire earth, the light of a single person living a godly life will serve to lighten the surroundings, and it will be the inextinguishable light of Christ shining through. Jesus said:

> *"…If they persecuted Me, they will also persecute you…"*   John 15:20

Remember: godless, secular society is hostile towards Christ, because Christian standards that are based upon true biblical teaching are in opposition to the world's system and standards—and we know who rules that from Day 8's reading!

There is one thing that holds back God's direct intervention and judgment in the world we live in, and that is His desire for the salvation of souls. You see, Christ came into this world to save sinners; that was His ultimate purpose. It was not to establish a perfect world, because Satan already had legitimate rule over it. Instead, He came to destroy the power and works of the devil and release man from bondage to sin — and all this Jesus achieved!

Inasmuch then as the children have partaken of flesh and blood, He Himself likewise shared in the same, that through death He might destroy him who had the power of death, that is, the devil, and release those who through fear of death were all their lifetime subject to bondage.

Hebrews 2:14-15

If the end times point to anything, they point to the appearing of Christ coming for His own! Let us live therefore for Eternity, as sojourners in a world that is passing away. Let us live in similitude to Abraham who, not being content with this life only, instead looked for a city whose builder and maker was God! Remember, your heart is where your treasure is!

In living for Eternity here, our lives will be far more beneficial to others by helping and pointing them to Christ, both in word and by example. Our lives will be less selfish and more loving and caring towards others.

Jesus set His face like a flint towards Jerusalem (Luke 9:51), knowing He would be crucified, yet consumed with passion to save a lost mankind. He had Eternity in mind for us, and not this life only.

… who for the joy that was set before Him [Jesus] endured the cross…

Hebrews 12:2

Similarly, we as ambassadors for Christ can seek to do God's will in this world, reaping benefits for others in the next! This is our honour and privilege in serving Christ.

Remember, we have a tremendously important role as God's children in this life and not just the next!

LIFE APPLICATIONS

- The end times pose a challenge, as does living a godly life. Determine to follow the Lord faithfully in a world that increasingly does not want Him.

- By staying close to Him in prayer and study, we will experience the intimate presence of God that will reassure us that He is with us no matter what.

- The rewards in following Jesus are beyond our minds comprehension; His peace will keep us through trouble, and He will never fail.

A PRAYER

I ask You, Lord, to help me trust You more every day instead of leaning on my own understanding regarding problems in my life. Instead, strengthen me to overcome, and make Your way clear before me, guiding me into all truth.

DAY 17

Living in the Last Days —
A Godly Life:
Living Responsibly and Uprightly Before God

*For the grace of God that brings salvation has appeared to all men, teaching us that, denying ungodliness and worldly lusts, we should live soberly, righteously, and **godly** in the present age, looking for the blessed hope and glorious appearing of our great God and Saviour Jesus Christ.*

Titus 2:11-13

Jesus never encouraged his followers to grow their roots too deep into this world, which is passing away! After performing the miracle of loaves and fishes for the five thousand, all the people sought after Jesus and flocked around Him, but Jesus had this to say to them:

Jesus answered them and said, "Most assuredly, I say to you, you seek Me, not because you saw the signs, but because you ate of the loaves and were filled. Do not labour for the food which perishes, but for the food which endures to everlasting life, which the Son of Man will give you, because God the Father has set His seal on Him."
…"For I have come down from heaven, not to do My own will, but the will of Him who sent Me. This is the will of the Father who sent Me, that of all He has given Me I should lose nothing, but should raise it up at the last day. And this is the will of Him who sent Me, that everyone who sees the Son and believes in Him may have everlasting life; and I will raise him up at the last day."

John 6:26-40

Here, Jesus makes His mission very clear to those who were seeking help for this world only and were not interested in the real purpose of His mission, which was to save them for all eternity.

"I am the bread of life," Jesus proclaimed. "He who comes to Me shall never hunger, and he who believes in Me shall never thirst."

They did not understand that Jesus was on a mission from His Heavenly Father. Jesus did not do or say as He pleased, because He knew He was sent to do the Father's will—to accomplish an eternal work of redemption that would secure man's needs forever!

This is the crunch: either to believe the Word of God and live the kind of Godly life He desires or to follow the world, enjoying the fruits of sin for a season. If I crave the things of the world, I shall sadly discover that they do not satisfy and, in fact, only lead to massive disappointment, disillusionment and emptiness! God created me with a spirit that only He can satisfy.

The crowds tasted the loaves and fishes and wanted more where they came from! This Jesus could solve all their food shortage problems! Is this not a problem of today's society—that we seek pleasures in this life more than God? The world is passing away, and yet we can live our lives as though we will live on earth forever!

As mentioned, Jesus was separated to doing the Father's will above all else, and He had much to say to his followers about their attitudes towards the world we live in. In substance, Jesus pointed to the right choices to make:

...seek first the kingdom of God and His righteousness, and all these things shall be added to you. Matthew 6:33

If then you were raised with Christ, seek those things which are above, where Christ is, sitting at the right hand of God. Set your mind on things above, not on things on the earth. Colossians 3:1-2

Clearly, our focus should always be upon pleasing God in our lives and not pleasing ourselves.

We are pleasing to God when we carry out our earthly commitments and responsibilities. For example, parents are responsible for their children and for a large season in their lives will need to be committed to that service as to God. It would be quite erroneous to suppose otherwise, for children are a heritage from the Lord and prospective members of the Kingdom of God. Children are loaned to parents to nurture in the ways of the Lord and prepare them for adult life, both physically and spiritually. What a ministry for the Lord this is!

Much more could be said regarding our commitment to life and all the responsibilities it brings.

Here is another example. To live within your means is actually living with integrity, responsibility, and godliness, for in doing so we learn to be patient, honest, upright, and content in all we have. We keep ourselves from the extreme, unwise addictions, such as living off a credit card, spending money we have not worked for! In this life, we need money to live. It is our duty and responsibility, therefore, to work with our hands and not be idle.

Let him who stole steal no longer, but rather let him labour, working with his hands what is good, that he may have something to give him who has need. Ephesians 4:28

Very often these tasks can be laborious and unexciting for the modern day we live in but are, nevertheless, essential for reasons we may not always be aware of! It is our attitude towards work and all our earthly duties and commitments that God uses to develop character. Further, He uses each one of us to minister and shine for Him in the world wherever people are found — and they are found in places of work!

True spirituality requires good, tried, proven character if a person is to be entrusted with the things of God! Let us never underestimate the place of work. "Approved character" lists after "perseverance" in the ladder of righteous and godly living!

And not only that, but we also glory in tribulations, knowing that tribulation produces perseverance; and perseverance, **character**; *and character, hope.* Romans 5:3-4

LIFE APPLICATIONS

THOUGHT FOR THE DAY

Now godliness with contentment is great gain.

*For we brought nothing into this world, and it is certain we
can carry nothing out. And having food and clothing, with
these we shall be content. But those who desire to be rich fall
into temptation and a snare, and into many foolish and
harmful lusts which drown men
in destruction and perdition.*

*For the love of money is a root of all kinds of evil, for which
some have strayed from the faith in their greediness,
and pierced themselves through with many sorrows.*

*But you, O man of God, flee these things and pursue
righteousness, godliness, faith, love, patience, gentleness.*

1 Timothy 6:6-11

DAY 18

Living in the Last Days—
A Godly Life: Christlike

For the grace of God that brings salvation has appeared to all men, teaching us that, denying ungodliness and worldly lusts, we should live soberly, righteously, and **godly** *in the present age, looking for the blessed hope and glorious appearing of our great God and Saviour Jesus Christ.*

Titus 2:11-13

... great is the mystery **of godliness:**
God was manifested in the flesh...

1 Timothy 3:16

This is an amazing Scripture, for:

- God has defined godliness in the example of our Lord Jesus Christ.
- Believers are to conform to Christ as an act of faithful obedience.
- Through our knowledge of Him, we grow in godliness.

All people born into this world, a world that is full of depravation and wickedness, are completely lost, destined for an endless, Godless eternity...

But then, right into its midst, in the fullness of times, Christ came—the indisputable Saviour of the world—to destroy the works of the devil and save a lost mankind! Beyond all doubt, beyond all question, the purpose of this "divine visitation" was to produce godliness in the hearts and lives of sinful mankind in a way and manner that was completely and deliberately withheld — until, that is, the fullness of time, and then Christ came!

But when the fullness of the time had come, God sent forth His Son, born of a woman, born under the law.
Galatians 4:4

After Christ's mission on this earth was complete, the headlines — across the whole realm of heaven, but not upon earth — were sounded! Angels marvelled as their Lord of Hosts entered heaven at His resurrection from the dead. They beheld their Lord clothed in humility as He returned, His body displaying the scars of "war" where soldiers had marred it. They must have witnessed the glory of God and pleasure of His Father welcoming Him home!

Lift up your heads, O you gates!
And be lifted up, you everlasting doors!
And the King of glory shall come in.
Who is this King of glory?
The Lord strong and mighty,
The Lord mighty in battle.
Lift up your heads, O you gates!
Lift up, you everlasting doors!
And the King of glory shall come in.
Who is this King of glory?
The Lord of hosts,
He is the King of glory. Selah.
Psalm 24:7-10

According to this Scripture, there must have been great excitement in heaven, for it could never have entered our heads or remotely come near to our human understanding just what God has prepared for those who love Him! This love — shed abroad in our hearts by the Holy Spirit — is received after embracing for oneself the understanding of this mystery now unfolded, Christ in us the hope of glory! Yes! Upon receiving Christ as our personal Lord and Saviour, the eternal Christ comes to dwell in us by the eternal Spirit of God!

… "Eye has not seen, nor ear heard, Nor have entered into the heart of man The things which God has prepared for those who love Him." But God has revealed them to us through His Spirit…   1 Corinthians 2:9-10

God was manifest in the flesh in the person of Christ, the Son of the Living God; and through the Holy Spirit, each believing heart can receive the illumination for themselves that these things are indeed true! As already declared, the Holy Spirit has been sent to each open heart with the purpose of revealing the things of God, thus making them alive and real to the believer! He provides within you the evidence of things not seen — a key ingredient of faith according to Hebrews 11:1.

The Holy Spirit speaks of life! Jesus is alive! This is the message!

Where the Spirit of the Lord is there is liberty! He has come to prepare us for Heaven through the Word of God and the blood of the Lamb, revealing Christ to us and transforming us into the same image from glory to glory!

Further, He has come to equip us, meanwhile, for

the battle that lies ahead—a battle involving both our flesh within and spiritual warfare without! The need to overcome can only increase as the time draws near. Yes! The battle will rage. And yet, the Bible says that in all these things, we are more than conquerors through Him Who loved us!

LIFE APPLICATIONS

- The sheer zeal and energy of the Holy Spirit demands my all and nothing less in the light of what Christ has achieved for me.

- I must be born again according to the words of Jesus in John 3:3—that is, born of the Spirit!

- "Do not marvel," said Jesus. In other words, do not be surprised at me telling you this: you must be born again!

DAY 19

Living in the Last Days —
A Godly Life: Christ in You!

*For the grace of God that brings salvation has appeared to all men, teaching us that, denying ungodliness and worldly lusts, we should live soberly, righteously, and **godly** in the present age, looking for the blessed hope and glorious appearing of our great God and Saviour Jesus Christ.*

Titus 2:11-13

*… great is the mystery **of godliness**:*
God was manifested in the flesh…

1 Timothy 3:16

It is not called a "mystery" because it is difficult to understand, but rather because it was formerly a divine secret but is now, in the New Testament, a fully disclosed truth for understanding and application. It was, if you like, a hidden truth but is now a revealed secret!

*[T]he mystery which has been hidden from ages and from generations, but now has been revealed to His saints. To them God willed to make known what are the riches of the glory of this mystery among the Gentiles: which is **Christ in you**, the hope of glory.*   Colossians 1:26-27

This is wonderfully described here as something God willed to be made known to His saints, not unlike a loving eager father desiring to see his children open the wrappings of his gift and discover openly what was previously hidden from them! Indeed, the "gift" of God in the person of Jesus Christ is pronounced as "His indescribable gift" in 2 Corinthians 9:15.

Godliness has now been revealed in Christ to the world, because "God was manifest in the flesh!" Jesus Christ, by His life, has revealed what God is like, how He thinks and lives, His righteousness and Holiness, and most importantly for our sakes, His Salvation for all mankind!

If this was a mystery not fully disclosed in times past, so also was the concept of God dwelling in man! Jesus, having died upon the cross to redeem sinful man and set him free from its power, now dwells in those who come to God through Him in the Person of the Holy Spirit! Never before has this privilege been available to all flesh through repentance — indeed, to the "whosoever" according to John 3:16!

The Jews at the time of Christ did not understand this truth, yet God revealed to Peter this mystery that the Gentiles were also called to the same body and privileges as the Jews. God arranged for Peter to visit a man called Cornelius, a Roman Centurion, to preach unto him and all his household.

Then Peter opened his mouth and said: "In truth I perceive that God shows no partiality. But in every nation whoever fears Him and works righteousness is accepted by Him.   Acts 10:34-35

While Peter was still speaking these words, the Holy Spirit fell upon all those who heard the word. And those of the circumcision who believed were astonished, as many as came with Peter, because the gift of the Holy Spirit had been poured out on the Gentiles also. For they heard them speak with tongues and magnify God.

Then Peter answered, "Can anyone forbid water, that these should not be baptized who have received the Holy Spirit just as we have?" And he commanded them to be baptized in the name of the Lord... Acts 10:44-48

Upon returning to Jerusalem, Peter had to explain to those of the circumcision (the Jews) why he had entered the house of a Gentile; and they, upon hearing Peter's account of all that God had done, became silent and glorified God saying, "Then God has also granted to the Gentiles repentance to life." (Acts 11:18)

The first coming of Christ into this world has changed everything. All events in this life are now pointing towards that day when Christ shall come again at His Second Coming, but this time in power and great glory, bringing with Him both reward and judgement.

Jesus Christ has been chosen by God to deliver both life and judgement to mankind, because He is the Son of Man.

For the Father judges no one, but has committed all judgment to the Son, that all should honour the Son just as they honour the Father. He who does not honour the Son does not honour the Father who sent Him.

Most assuredly, I say to you, he who hears My word and believes in Him who sent Me has everlasting life, and shall not come into judgment, but has passed from death into life.
John 5:22-24

Most assuredly, I say to you, the hour is coming, and now is, when the dead will hear the voice of the Son of God; and those who hear will live. For as the Father has life in

Himself, so He has granted the Son to have life in Himself, and has given Him authority to execute judgment also, because He is the Son of Man. Do not marvel at this; for the hour is coming in which all who are in the graves will hear His voice and come forth – those who have done good, to the resurrection of life, and those who have done evil, to the resurrection of condemnation.   John 5:25-29

We are, therefore, to live a Godly life in this world if we are to victoriously overcome what lies ahead, for indeed it will be a life of spiritual warfare and battling through the last days as a soldier of Christ, living in His blood-bought victory. This is an essential part of our calling, and now we know what godliness entails, for God has defined it.

- **God has defined godliness in the example of our Lord Jesus Christ.**
- **Believers are to conform to Christ as an act of faithful obedience.**
- **Through our knowledge of Him, we grow in godliness.**

This, remember, is our ultimate calling—to be like Christ. As He has overcome, so shall we. By following His example and giving full allegiance to obeying His Word.

And they overcame him by the blood of the Lamb and by the word of their testimony, and they did not love their lives to the death.   Revelation 12:11

LIFE APPLICATIONS

A PRAYER

Dear Lord, I realise that my life and purpose is to live the way you desire for me and not to do my own thing.
Thank you, Lord.
I come now to trust you for my life and my future. Amen.

DAY 20

Living in the Last Days —
Looking for the Blessed Hope and Glorious
Appearing of Our Great God and Saviour Jesus Christ

*For the grace of God that brings salvation has appeared to all men, teaching us that, denying ungodliness and worldly lusts, we should live soberly, righteously, and godly in the present age, **looking for the blessed hope and glorious appearing of our great God and Saviour Jesus Christ.***

Titus 2:11-13

Have you noticed, whilst looking at the above passage of Scripture every day since Day 10, that everything in this verse is pointing to one event — *looking for the blessed hope and glorious appearing of our great God and Saviour Jesus Christ!*

There is another verse of Scripture that is relevant here, and it could easily rest alongside this and follow on from it. It is found in 1 John 3:2-3 and reads:

*Beloved, now we are children of God; and it has not yet been revealed what we shall be, but we know that when He is revealed, we shall be like Him, for we shall see Him as He is. **And everyone who has this hope in Him purifies himself, just as He is pure.***

This tells us clearly that those who have this "hope within them" and are looking for Christ's coming will keep themselves **pure** just as He is pure. The prospect of being transformed into the likeness of Christ when we see Him at His coming is intended to motivate Christians to live righteously. Yet, how much are we taught about Christ's second coming, given that this is the focus that motivates us into keeping ourselves pure?

Christ's ability to overcome temptation and remain pure makes Him the perfect example to follow. Throughout our sojourning in this world, we can rest assured that with the Spirit of Christ dwelling within us as born-again believers, we shall have all the power necessary to overcome, just as He overcame, and consequently live a victorious life in Him.

The fact is, all the power of the Godhead dwells in Christ, and He dwells in us! The Bible confirms this and reassures us by saying:

For in Him dwells all the fullness of the Godhead bodily; and you are complete in Him…
Colossians 2:9-10

You are of God, little children, and have overcome them, because He who is in you is greater than he who is in the world.
1 John 4:4

Regarding the Second Coming of our Lord Jesus Christ, the fact is that only the Father knows when this long-awaited event will be. This is purposely designed to move and motivate every believer into committing their life to Christ daily to do His will. We neither know the day nor the hour of His coming, and so it is for this very reason that we should face each day as though it were the day that Jesus could come — today! It would be quite false to say otherwise, because the truth is that we just don't know when it will be — and so, it could be today!

Of course, the Bible gives us signs and indicators, telling us there will be wars and rumours of wars, famines, pestilences, and earthquakes—but have these not already happened in abundance?

Once again, it is the Book of 1 John that guides us practically in this matter of how we should live in readiness for His coming.

*And now, little children, **abide in Him**, that when He appears, we may have confidence and not be ashamed before Him at His coming.* 1 John 2:28

This shows how important it is to **abide in Christ**. It is this abiding union with Jesus that brings forth the necessary fruits of Christlikeness. Abiding in Christ speaks of my personal relationship with Him as both Lord and Saviour, but it is important to remember that this primarily involves submission to Him through obedience to His Word.

*If you abide in Me, and **My words abide in you**, you will ask what you desire, and it shall be done for you.* John 15:7

*As the Father loved Me, I also have loved you; abide in My love. **If you keep My commandments, you will abide in My love**, just as I have kept My Father's commandments and abide in His love.* John 15:9-10

The importance of obedience to God can never be over-emphasised. It is better than all sacrifices, as King Saul discovered long ago in 1 Samuel 15:22.

…"Has the Lord as great delight in burnt offerings and sacrifices, As in obeying the voice of the Lord? Behold, to obey is better than sacrifice, And to heed than the fat of rams."

Obedience to God will ensure we abide in His love.

In fact, obedience is a vital tool in God's toolbox for the days leading up to His coming. It will ensure my life is under His protection. Life is a spiritual battle each day, both within as well as without, but by abiding in Christ, we are fellowshipping with the One Who has been given all power in heaven and earth.

Remember,

You are of God, little children, and have overcome them, because He who is in you is greater than he who is in the world.   1 John 4:4

LIFE APPLICATIONS

- Do I have a personal relationship with Christ, and am I abiding in Him? If so, can I truly say, in accordance with John 15:7, that His words abide in me?

A PRAYER

I realise that your divine programme in this world is working towards the Second Coming of Christ. Help me, Lord, to know your presence in my life daily, as I seek to honour and obey you so that I may experience a personal walk with you.

PART 3

DAY 21

Living in the Last Days — Faith: How Much?

*…the just shall live by… **faith.***

Habakkuk 2:4

What is required of each one of us, if we are to have victory in Christ? It is **faith** in His Word.

> *For whatever is born of God overcomes the world. And this is the victory that has overcome the world – our faith.*

1 John 5:4

We have the power of God available, because we are the redeemed of God, His children. But this power to overcome and defeat the enemy can only be appropriated as I trust and affirm God's Word personally in my own life. Remember Jesus when tempted by the devil?

The spirit of the world is in opposition to God, but when we determine to stand, by faith in God's Word, the world loses its controlling influence over us.

Today's thoughts are to lead us into thinking about faith and how this plays an essential and vital role in these last days.

Some people feel that they have little faith, rather like the disciples in the fishing boat when a sudden storm raged against it, threatening their lives and filling them with fear. Look at Jesus' response:

But He said to them, "Why are you fearful, O you of little faith?" Then He arose and rebuked the winds and the sea, and there was a great calm. So the men marveled, saying, "Who can this be, that even the winds and the sea obey Him?"

Matthew 8:26-27

This reply by our Lord Jesus is worth thinking about. The disciples in the boat on the stormy sea were followers of Jesus; and though their faith may have been small, nevertheless, Jesus expected more from them!

"Little faith" in the original Greek means "small faith" and describes a faith that lacks confidence or trusts too little. Jesus used the word in various situations as a tender rebuke or corrective chiding. (See Matthew 6:30, 8:26, 14:31, 16:8 and Luke 12:28)

Another way to think of this is as "undeveloped faith" as opposed to outright unbelief or distrust.

To exercise faith is a choice and requires a denying of our own reasoning and a trust in God. Whether we have small faith or large faith is, in a sense, not the issue; the process of faith can still be applied according to the quality and measure of faith we have.

Jesus told His disciples that if they had faith "as a mustard seed" they could move mountains.

Upon this occasion, the disciples were unable to cast out a demon.

Then the disciples came to Jesus privately and said, "Why could we not cast it out?"

So Jesus said to them, "Because of your unbelief; for assuredly, I say to you, if you have faith as a mustard seed, you will say to this mountain, 'Move from here to there,' and it will move; and nothing will be impossible for you."

Matthew 17:19-20

Jesus calls faith a seed. Now, a seed has great potential, but it does not become a tree overnight. It needs to be planted in good soil to be activated, and then it will grow! Faith in God starts in a similar way. When we put our faith into action — putting the seed into the ground — that is when we release it to God. What happens next is a miracle in the making, just as the seed planted in good soil becomes a stalk, then develops into a sapling, and then a tree!

In this passage, Jesus shows us the way to see our mountains removed.

First, God says we all have a measure of faith —

*For I say, through the grace given to me, to everyone who is among you, not to think of himself more highly than he ought to think, but to think soberly, as God has dealt to each one a **measure of faith**.*   Romans 12:3

This "measure of faith" is resident within you and was put there by God when you first received Christ.

Second, God says this faith comes alive by "hearing the Word of God."

So then faith comes by hearing, and hearing by the word of God.   Romans 10:17

Third, God says that you can apply your faith to see your daily needs met. How? You do something as an act of your faith. You sow the mustard seed of your faith into an action. Then, when your faith has been planted and is growing, speak to your mountain and watch God set about its removal. Remember, God is an abundant

God Who gives us far more than we ask or think. As you give your total self to God, so God gives of His endless blessings to you.

Faith that appears small or weak to us can still accomplish the humanly impossible. The "mountain" spoken of by Jesus is a metaphor for an obstacle, hindrance, or humanly insurmountable problem. God can deal with "mountains" through the faith of people committed to Him who accurately understand and know His power, will, purposes and provision for their lives.

But without faith it is impossible to please Him, for he who comes to God must believe that He is, and that He is a rewarder of those who diligently seek Him.   Hebrews 11:6

Jesus expects to see faith in action according to the measure given to us at any given time. In the light of this, we can never be excused for thinking that our "little faith" may be insufficient to do what God requires of us. We cannot, as believers, relinquish ourselves from all responsibility to yield our lives to God in service and full commitment, simply because we don't feel good enough, worthy enough, or more to the point, because we feel we have insufficient faith!

LIFE APPLICATIONS

- God gave me a measure of faith when I became born again, and I can rest assured that this faith can work miracles if I put it into practice daily.

- We should always remember that God is for us and not against us. Let us re-dedicate our lives to Him today and learn to walk by faith with a God Who desires the best for us.

DAY 22

Living in the Last Days — Childlike Faith

*…the just shall live by… **faith**.*

Habakkuk 2:4

Upon occasions, Jesus turned to the simple faith of little children to make a statement. A little child trusts and believes unreservedly and unconditionally. It is this quality, found in small children, that I believe Jesus is looking for in each one of us who professes to believe in Him — to have a trusting, childlike faith!

… "Assuredly, I say to you, unless you are converted and become as little children, you will by no means enter the kingdom of heaven."
Matthew 18:3

Here Jesus stipulates that the way into the Kingdom of Heaven is by the simple trust and dependence of a child; and the way to greatness in the Kingdom is by the humility of a child.

Interestingly, the word *humbles* literally means "to make low." It describes a person who is devoid of all arrogance and self-exultation, a person who is willingly submitted to God and His will.

The tendency of humankind is opposite to that of this childlikeness and humility. Man chooses to serve his own interests. His idea of power and authority is to be dominant and controlling over others. "Not so," says Jesus. In the Kingdom of God, we are called to childlike humility and a servant-like heart! In this manner, Jesus defines the spirt and style by which the authority of a believer is to be exercised as that of an ambassador of Christ and a representative of God's kingdom power on earth.

> *Then little children were brought to Him that He might put His hands on them and pray, but the disciples rebuked them. But Jesus said, "Let the little children come to Me, and do not forbid them; for of such is the kingdom of heaven." And He laid His hands on them…*
>
> Matthew 19:13-15

We should give attention to the fact that Jesus often referred to little children in His ministry, and here is another passage where He singles them out to emphasise an important point regarding the nature of those who are in the Kingdom of Heaven!

Jesus was again pointing to the simple faith little children have in trusting and receiving. He inferred that the Kingdom of God is only for those who come to Him with the humble dependence and trust of little children — that is, in simple faith.

A deeper implication here is that God deliberately chooses to give His kingdom to such; it belongs to them, not because of merit, but because God wills to give it to the humble and the apparently insignificant or unimportant. This is consistent with God's approval of Christ Who, having humbled Himself even to death on a cross, was highly exalted and given a name above all others!

> *And being found in appearance as a man, He **humbled** Himself and became obedient to the point of death, even the death of the cross. Therefore God also has highly exalted Him and given Him the name which is above every name, that at*

the name of Jesus every knee should bow, of those in heaven, and of those on earth, and of those under the earth, and that every tongue should confess that Jesus Christ is Lord, to the glory of God the Father.   Philippians 2:8-11

In fact, the Bible is very clear; God gives grace to the humble but resists the proud! This is so important to recognise and take on board as Christians, so we should take stock of our lives daily and walk humbly before our Lord with this new perspective of life engrained into our innermost being, always looking to Jesus as the perfect example to follow in humility!

So, childlike humility is an important trait in the Kingdom of God! The awesomeness of God's Person alone should perhaps itself warrant this from His children who are but dust in comparison to His eternal, omnipotent, majestic being whose appearance shines with blinding light! Whilst this is of course true — that we are such in comparison to God — yet we must never forget how He loves us and has desired from eternity that we should live with Him in His Kingdom forever!

Let us never forget that God's values each individual enough to warrant the death of His Own Son!

LIFE APPLICATIONS

- Does the thought of being childlike towards God regarding matters of trust and faith seem somewhat inappropriate or condescending to you, just as it was with the disciples when they saw parents bringing children to Jesus?

- When considering what we read and see regarding the character and Person of our Lord Jesus Christ — that He is the Creator of the universe and the eternal Son of God, yet gave Himself for each one of us — is it such a hard thing to humble ourselves before Him and go forth in the power of His Spirit to be a witness of light?

- Do I have a close personal relationship with God? A distant relationship with God?

DAY 23

Living in the Last Days — Faith Leads to Life

*...the just shall **live by**... **faith.***

Habakkuk 2:4

What is your perception of being alive and living life to the full? Before we can look at living by faith, we must address life itself and our expectations of it.

The Hebrew word for "live" in Habakkuk 2:4 means: to stay alive, be preserved, flourish, enjoy life, live in happiness, be alive and breath!

The Bible talks about a certain industrious man who worked very hard and built a large, profitable business. This probably consumed most of his time and completely occupied his life. However, a divine law stating that "what a man sows, that shall he reap" applied, and in this case the man, through his hard work, reaped much in earthly goods. Now, he decided in his heart to pull down his barns and build bigger barns so that he would have much stored away for himself later in life. After doing this, it became his philosophy to eat, drink and be merry for he perceived that he had many goods laid up for the future! Unfortunately, the man soon died and could not benefit from anything!

This parable was spoken by our Lord, and it is found in Luke 12:16-21. The point being made by Jesus was this:

*And He said to them, "Take heed and beware of covetousness, for one's **life** does not consist in the abundance of the things he possesses."*

Luke 12:15

Notice that God did not condemn the man because of all the hard work he did! He was denounced for the following reasons:

But God said to him, 'Fool! This night your soul will be required of you; then whose will those things be which you have provided?'
So is he who lays up treasure for himself, and is not rich toward God.

It is imperative, when considering one's expectations in life, to look at what life does not consist of as spoken by Jesus: **one's life does not consist in the abundance of the things he possesses.**

It is a lie and ultimately foolish to think that my life would be happier **if only I had much more money than I have now!**

Consequently, we need to see what the Bible teaches us about life and what life does consist of!

The Bible suggests that **true living** is the direct result of doing the right thing.

A passage in the Old testament, when God spoke to His people prior to their entering the Promised Land, confirms this.

*See, I have set before you today **life** and good, death and evil, in that I command you today to love the Lord your God, to walk in His ways, and to keep His commandments, His statutes, and His judgments, **that you may live** and multiply; and the Lord your God will bless you in the land which you go to possess… I call heaven and earth as witnesses today against you, that I have set before you **life** and death, blessing and cursing; therefore **choose life**, that both you and your descendants **may live**; that you may love the Lord your*

*God, that you may obey His voice, and that you may cling to Him, for **He is your life and the length of your days**…*
Deuteronomy 30:15, 19-20

The words "live" and "life" appear six times in the above passage. These promises clearly show us the way to live a true, full life—a life that will be blessed by God—and yet, because God has given us free will, we must choose! Nevertheless, it is obvious that God, our Creator, knows what is best for us. This is where your faith comes in! Do you—do I—really believe that God knows best for me?

See how God authoritatively declares His promises to those who will yield their lives to keeping His Word as they enter life in a new land:

- *… I command you today to love the Lord your God, to walk in His ways…that you **may live** and multiply*

- *… and the Lord your God will **bless you** in the land which you go to possess*

- *… therefore **choose life,** that both you and your descendants may **live***

- *…**He is your life and the length of your days***

This Word is full of promises made by God towards His people. It is just as applicable today as you enter life with God. God knows you personally—and your life and destiny; after all, He created each one of us.

What we can easily forget or fail to appreciate is that God Himself is our life. He created us that way! We were made to live a life with God forever!

Now, of course, the serpent in the garden convinced Adam and Eve otherwise so that we are all born with a human nature that does not know God or desire His fellowship! Yet, the irony is this: nothing else will satisfy us! He takes us on paths that will lead to real life, and we will ultimately be blessed of the Lord.

How imperative it is, therefore, that in the last days, when there will be perilous times, we keep His commandments and live!

LIFE APPLICATIONS

- Can I truly say that I am living by faith?

- Life is short! What is the most important thing in my life?

A PRAYER

Lord, help me to recognise those things in life that are most important and be less consumed with all the rest.
May I always seek Your righteousness first and Your Kingdom purposes. You said in Matthew 6:33 that all these things shall be added to me if I put You first.

DAY 24

Living in the Last Days — Life is Short

*…the just shall **live by**… **faith.***

Habakkuk 2:4

In my younger years, a certain passage of Scripture spoke to me in a very enlightening manner regarding the length and duration of my life. It was this:

> *Come now, you who say, "Today or tomorrow we will go to such and such a city, spend a year there, buy and sell, and make a profit"; whereas you do not know what will happen tomorrow. **For what is your life? It is even a vapor that appears for a little time and then vanishes away.** Instead you ought to say, "If the Lord wills, we shall live and do this or that."*

James 4:13-15

One year, on Bonfire Night, we held a church social that many young people attended. Near the end, I was asked to bring a short epilogue from God's Word to close. The occasion was, by its very nature, a smoky one! I decided to illustrate the above passage of Scripture in a manner that I considered to be appropriate. I hung up a piece of string then lit the bottom of it with a match. As the flame took light and climbed vertically up the string, I immediately stubbed it out so that it smouldered, creating a lot of smoke. I then asked the question, "Where does the smoke come from, and where is it going?"

The answer to either of these questions was not clear or obvious. The smoke vanished away into "thin air," as we often say, so we could not say just where it had gone.

I went on to say that life was a little bit like that. We are born into this world knowing nothing about it; then, we leave it quickly after three score and ten years (perhaps a lot more or a lot less), seemingly vanishing away at death. I then posed the question:

"For what is your life? It is even a vapor — like the smoke — that appears for a little time and then vanishes away."   James 4:14

I went on to give another Scripture that came to mind:

And the world is passing away, and the lust of it; but he who does the will of God abides forever.
1 John 2:17

The point being made was the need for each one to surrender to God's purposes for their life and not wander aimlessly in this world. The time of opportunity is limited; indeed, it is very short. (The duration of the smoke hanging in the air and then disappearing out of sight brought this home quite vividly!)

Afterwards, we prayed and that was that.

As the people dispersed to go home, one young man, about nineteen years of age, stood still, gazing at me thoughtfully. He walked over to me and said something to the effect of, "I wish to give my life to God. I want to do His will — something with real purpose. I feel my life at present has no purpose."

God had spoken to him that evening, and as a result he ended what he considered to be a mundane job and entered full-time service and training for a Christian organisation.

It is a wonderful thing when a person experiences the call of God upon their life! And to observe it before your very eyes is awesome! I will never forget that young man.

Today's title — *Life is Short* — is so true, and yet without God enlightening our eyes to see the real picture, we remain deluded, thinking and behaving as though we will never die but live forever!

"I am young and have all my life ahead of me," one might think, when really the truth is that by God's grace and His will, I do!

God's grace is the only hope we have in this life — as well as the next. He knows the length of our days. God's calling and will for each one of us is to do those good works He has ordained for us to do.

For we are His workmanship, created in Christ Jesus for good works, which God prepared beforehand that we should walk in them. Ephesians 2:10

A young relative of mine decided to train and become a chef; it seemed attractive at the time, and she enjoyed food preparation and all that it entailed. But then, having become qualified and tried two different jobs, she declined them both! Why? Here's what she said:

"It's not what I really wish to do — well, not for the rest of my life!" She walked away thoughtfully and considered within her heart what to do, then finally came up with a different purpose and vision altogether!

"I want to help people and care for them; I want to go back to college and study for a qualification in Care."

This desire did not originate in her head, but in her heart. To this very day, many years later, she will tell me, "I love my job!"

This time her work was something she could do all her life! Now she is head-hunted and holds a senior practitioner position in Social Care; she loves working with elderly people, assessing and prescribing their individual care needs. She is not just doing a job but is motivated from within to do it with a passion and genuine concern for each person, with a love that God Himself put there!

A THOUGHTFUL MEDITATION

- By faith, I believe God's Word that He has prepared good works for me to do — His works.

- By faith, I believe that I stand in a space where no one else stands, That there are things God has put within me that are unique for me alone to do!

A PRAYER

Lord, life is short. I yield myself to You, desiring to know Your purpose for me.

Living in the Last Days — Faith: Applying God's Word

*…the just shall **live** by… faith.*

Habakkuk 2:4

If ever we are to truly live by faith in this world, it will only be by applying God's Word. Nothing else is reliable; our own inclinations, desires and ambitions can lead to a dismal end, leaving us dissatisfied and disgruntled, discovering they were not the perfect solution to happiness.

If I do not truly believe that God's Word is the very substance and essential ingredient of my life, then I will inevitably at some point along the way turn aside to my own understanding, choosing my own way and assessment of things. It is often said we must learn by our mistakes and grow from our misfortunes, and in part this is true; but some mistakes can lead to grave outcomes, and if they can be avoided, all the better!

Perhaps this is one of the hardest lessons of all. I am created with free will to make choices and decisions, and this will always be the case. Yet, as a fallen being, I need the guiding hand of God in my life. Because God loves me, He respects this freedom of choice He has given me. However, the truth is, I do not know what is best for me, and my own reasoning will all too often be influenced by selfish desires, blind illusions, and unrealistic expectations. When I begin to realise that God created me uniquely in His own image, put within me His giftings, and has a plan for my life, then I will boldly choose to walk by faith, putting my trust in His Word. I will choose to rest my decisions upon His Word, guidance and leading. This will work!

The following Scripture is a favourite to remember:

Trust in the Lord with all your heart,
And lean not on your own understanding;
In all your ways acknowledge Him,
And He shall direct your paths.

Proverbs 3:5-6

Here it tells us that our own understanding is unreliable, and therefore God simply wants to be there for us! If we acknowledge Him, consult Him, pray to Him about everything, He has promised to direct us!

King David in the Old Testament was a man who reverently feared God and was very aware of his own limitations. Before going out to war against an enemy, he would consult God first by asking, "Will you deliver the enemy into my hand if I go into battle? Should I go out against them?"

As King over Israel, David could have made these decisions himself; after all, he was in charge. And yet, he chose to ask God instead, a decision that always saved the day. He knew that, ultimately, he could not see the situation perfectly and realised that there may have been unexpected hazards and dangers lying in wait. He knew God saw the true situation!

On at least one occasion David considered the enemy to be too strong for him to fight, but after consulting God, he was told to go forward in spite of the strength of the enemy; and even though David's armies were outnumbered, God would deliver them into his hand.

In a completely different scenario, the enemy may have been exceedingly small in number and the battle outcome seemingly obvious. David would still enquire of God, however, not leaning on his own understanding, and often God would instruct him not to go out to battle!

It is this absolute trust in God that always yields a successful outcome, for I can rarely see all that there is to see by my own understanding.

Living by faith in the last days requires us to exercise this kind of faith, and it necessitates an established trust through a personal relationship with God—a trust through a life of proving God and His Word to be true in our own lives.

Interestingly, it was David once again who, as a young teenager, learned what it meant to trust God and apply his faith.

He was responsible for watching over his father's sheep. One day, he saw a bear approaching the sheep, hunting for food. David went out to confront it and slew the bear! On another occasion he saw a lion approaching the flock, and again, in the same way, he killed the lion! It was quite possible that no one else saw this or ever knew anything about these exploits, as David was isolated and alone in the hills with his father's sheep, but birthed within him was a growing trust and faith in God that he had proved for himself. In his heart, David knew that it was God Who had helped him. We can all prove God for ourselves!

When the armies of Israel were challenged by the Philistine champion called Goliath, it was David's faith in God that won the day! Here is what David declared to King Saul upon that dramatic occasion:

> *Then David said to Saul, "Let no man's heart fail because of him; your servant will go and fight with this Philistine."*
>
> *And Saul said to David, "You are not able to go against this Philistine to fight with him; for you are a youth, and he a man of war from his youth."*
>
> *But David said to Saul, "Your servant used to keep his father's sheep, and when a lion or a bear came and took a lamb out of the flock, I went out after it and struck it, and delivered the lamb from its mouth; and when it arose against me, I caught it by its beard, and struck and killed it. Your servant has killed both lion and bear; and this uncircumcised Philistine will be like one of them, seeing he has defied the armies of the living God." Moreover David said, "The Lord, who delivered me from the paw of the lion and from the paw of the bear, He will deliver me from the hand of this Philistine."*
>
> 1 Samuel 17:32-37

The Holy Spirit is attentive to all those who put their trust and faith in Jesus. He will help us if we turn to God in prayer and are willing to take that initial step of faith, for He will bring God's promises to our remembrance. That's why it is so very important to read God's Word daily to know His promises. He will bring to my attention and remembrance whatever Scriptures I may have read or heard, even from the distant past. These words He will put into my mind that I might seize them and apply them, just like putting into action the sword of the Spirit against a spiritual enemy.

LIFE APPLICATIONS

- Would you describe your faith as passive or active?

- Faith may be described as activating God's Word — that is, believing it, trusting in it, obeying it, then looking for its fulfilment in your life. Do I often pray in a proactive manner like this?

THOUGHT

*...**faith** comes by hearing, and hearing by the **word of God***.

DAY 26

Living in the Last Days —
Justified by Faith: From the Very Beginning

…the just shall live by… faith.

Habakkuk 2:4

If you think about it for a moment, the very essence of how God justifies us is not a new thing.

We are, first, saved by His Grace alone through our faith in the finished work of the cross. Sin had to be dealt with, and the promise of a Saviour from the very beginning of time meant that its remedy was to come in Christ; His blood would atone for all sin and faith in "the blood of the Lamb" provided for God's mercy and grace throughout all ages. With this provision in mind, God looked for people who would essentially have faith in Him, believe and obey him. It is as I believe God and respond to obey His Word by faith that I become justified.

God, in the New Testament, tells me to repent and yield my life to Jesus Christ as my Lord and Saviour. As mentioned on Day 1, God has spoken to us in these last days by His Son! God gave us His only begotten Son and declared that whosoever believes in Him shall not perish but have everlasting life! If by faith I believe this decree made by the Father regarding His Son and, with the Holy Spirit's leading, turn aside to follow Him so that His Word becomes paramount in my life, then I shall be saved by grace through His shed blood and justified by my faith and acceptance of it.

The Old Testament vividly shows us how one man—Abraham—was justified by faith in God alone!

The Bible says that:

… "Abraham believed God, and it was accounted to him for righteousness."   Romans 4:3

By faith Abraham obeyed when he was called to go out to the place which he would receive as an inheritance. And he went out, not knowing where he was going. By faith he dwelt in the land of promise as in a foreign country, dwelling in tents with Isaac and Jacob, the heirs with him of the same promise;

These all died in faith, not having received the promises, but having seen them afar off were assured of them, embraced them and confessed that they were strangers and pilgrims on the earth.

… now they desire a better, that is, a heavenly country. Therefore God is not ashamed to be called their God…   Hebrews 11:8-9, 13, 16

It is here, at the beginning of the Bible before there was any law of Moses given, that we see faith in action!

Abraham obeyed God and went out towards a place that would be given to him as an inheritance. He went out, not knowing the way, but simply walking under God's directions by faith! Does this remind you of something? Does this not remind you of how we are called out by God to believe in Jesus Who is the way, the truth and the life? To follow Him as He takes us to a heavenly land?

A challenging circumstance early on in my life of following the Lord, which tested my faith to the limit, comes to mind.

My wife and I, with our then two young children, were living in lowly-rented accommodation in Acton, London. It essentially consisted of a mere two rooms; howbeit they were large rooms with partitions. There came a season when I looked for a job promotion that would take us out of London, preferably to the countryside! We were often pressurised by family to move. "After all, this is not the place to live and bring up children. Properties are far cheaper up in the North of England," they would say.

All applications for jobs thus far had failed until one came along which I seemed to qualify for perfectly. I really believed this to be the one to go for!

After praying about it, I did not feel at peace. I thought of going for the interview surmising that if it was not God's will, I wouldn't get it—but I did not feel any peace about that scenario either! I became so burdened about everything. After sharing all with my wife, I took the stamped, addressed job-application and tore it in two!

Peace flooded into me like a river! You see, we were in God's will right there in those two rooms. God did not wish us to move at that time; and certainly, He didn't take us away from London for a total of forty years, though eventually we did move to a different area! I saw the green fields of the countryside; God, at that time in our lives, saw differently!

This scenario reminded me of when Lot separated his sheep from those of Abraham, choosing to dwell in the lush fields of Sodom, whereas Abraham went to live in the desert! I remembered this story about Abraham very well. At the beginning of my walk with

God, I began reading the Bible from Genesis, having first read one Gospel previously. It seemed the best place to start at the time, and Abraham's life of faith spoke to me and helped me in those early days, showing me how to walk by faith with God. I knew I would rather be in the wilderness with God, than doing my own thing and possibly ending up in "Sodom" just like Lot!

My wife and I had both prayed about the job scenario, asking God to show us the way forward, and that's what He did!

We were attending a church nearby, where we received the Word of God and were engaged in ministry with children's work, teens leaders and the open-air outreaches. Most of all, we were receiving Bible study, which was to help us for the rest of our lives. I had also been given opportunities to preach and become an elder!

There are times when God wants us to put the interests of His Kingdom above everything else so that He can build us up and equip us for what lies ahead — and this was surely one of them. If we commit our way to Him, He has promised to direct our path. We simply have to trust Him with our lives.

At that time, God had already written upon my heart a Scripture that I heard preached on the first day I came to the Lord —

*Then Jesus said to His disciples, "If anyone desires to come after Me, let him deny himself, and take up his cross, and follow Me. For whoever desires to save his life will lose it, but whoever loses his life for My sake will find it. **For what profit is it to a man if he gains the whole world, and loses his own soul?** Or what will a man give in exchange for his soul?*
Matthew 16:24-26

This passage, being already engraved upon my very soul, meant that I feared to do anything outside of God's will. I wanted to go for the interview; I wanted to get a better job and leave London, preferring the country any day to city life—but not without God's blessing! I could not do it if the Lord was not with me! In the Old Testament, the people of Israel were not allowed to move camp unless the pillar of cloud moved first, and then—and only then—did they get up and go!

It can be very challenging to follow God, and my situation burdened me. There is always a tug between going God's way and going your own way! Yet, ultimately, there was no real obstacle; following God was everything to me, so I gladly tore up the letter and felt very relieved in doing so. I trusted that He knew better than I, and by faith both my wife and I carried on where we left off, only now at peace and full of joy knowing that we were in God's will and plan for our lives—and He was right there with us!

When I asked my children, later on in life, where the happiest place they had lived was, guess what their response was! It was when we all lived a simple life in Acton in those two rooms! You see, if children have a good loving relationship with their parents, they will prefer that to anything else and be content wherever they live.

Anyway, if God allowed His Son to be born in a stable, what could I complain about, living in two rooms?

There was an old song we used to sing in that church hall in Acton. It went something like:

What matters where on Earth we dwell, on mountain top or in the dell, in cottage or in mansion fair, where JESUS is 'tis Heaven there![iv]

We proved that obeying God and being in His will was all that mattered in life. He promised that if we sought His Kingdom first, all these other things would be added — and this we also proved.

After retiring and leaving London, having spent forty years in that city, we moved to Oxfordshire, joined a wonderful church, and carried on ministering.

Even as a born-again Christian, had I ignored the Holy Spirit's promptings and gone my own way then, I would have walked outside of God's will for my life! Learning obedience is an essential part of life as a child of God. I am saved at conversion — yes! — but I am being continually saved throughout my life, being taught, tested, and tried. Then, ultimately, I shall be saved when Christ comes, or He takes me!

LIFE APPLICATIONS

- Do I trust God enough with my whole life and all my plans and decisions?

A PRAYER

I know Lord in my heart that it must be wonderful to have that trust and faith in You… and yet, sometimes I seem to worry and grow fearful.
Forgive me, Lord. Help me to know You in a more personal way — Your love, companionship, and friendship.

DAY 27

Living in the Last Days — Faith that Works by Love

...the just shall live by... faith.

Habakkuk 2:4

Since beginning my walk with God in 1965, I have relied upon His Word to teach me, guide me, and direct me; and this continues now after fifty-two years down the line.

In the initial days I depended very much upon Him showing me things like a child — in pictures, dreams, even visions! I was not mature enough, knowing little of His Word. But what I did know was this: God was very real!

I was all alone as a student in London in those early days. One day, I asked a student pastor if he knew any Scriptures to do with "guidance." Like most young people, I was in a quandary as to what to do. You see, someone had told me that I should go and be a missionary as a teacher, and this troubled me for I had never thought about it like that. I realised, however, that the person had probably said that because I was coming to the end of my studies and this they considered to be a "good Christian opportunity." However, if I was going to do anything, then I needed God to show me personally.

The student pastor gave me the following verse:

I will instruct you and teach you in the way you should go; I will guide you with My eye.

Psalm 32:8

This became my personal, daily prayer request to God for a long time. He did not tell me to go abroad and be a missionary, as exciting as that may have been to some, but opened the way for me to be a lecturer in Further Education. This is what God wanted me to do, and over thirty-seven years I met with and spoke to thousands of students from all religions around the world. There are so many testimonies I could give, but I will speak of one.

At the end of one of my lectures, as the students were all leaving, I observed one particular student who happened to be a Sikh, full of bruises upon his face. As I sat at my desk, I beckoned him over to sit opposite me. When we were all alone, I asked him directly about his "face."

"Oh!" he said. "It was from a racial attack in the street."

I was moved with compassion for the student upon hearing this and told him I was sorry that he had experienced such a dreadful thing. My immediate reaction was to ask if he would like me to pray for him, for such a trauma must have inflicted other kinds of hurtful wounds and not just the physical. He gazed at me, and then, in a respectful manner, he said, "Yes please."

Afterwards, we shook hands and he left, looking much happier at having shared his experience with me. Thereafter, I had a friend for life! Whenever he saw me walking through the college grounds, he would stop and comment audibly with a loud "Thank you" in front of all his mates; then, with a smile on his face, he would walk over to me, shake my hand and carry on! I have rarely felt respected so much by anyone as I did at that time.

He was a walking testimony of just how "faith that works by love" can work and operate in us and through us to the world around—just were we happen to be. I don't know what God did exactly in that young man as I prayed for him that day, but it certainly hit him and affected him big-time!

The essence of God's calling is always to minister to and bless others. That is it! He knows the specifics of our giftings; He has already put them there! What we must do is walk in obedience, by faith that works by love, so that these "good works" will manifest themselves and come to fruition.

Life is always busy! Working. Bringing up children. Serving the Lord! As is so easy, you can sacrifice your personal time spent with God for works of service; and when you are seen to be conscientious and enthusiastic, you soon find increasing demands coming your way! It is good if you can discern exactly the specific work God desires you to do and give yourself wholeheartedly to that, remembering to balance your total commitments with other responsibilities in life too!

One day, I heard a guest preacher talk about "seeking the Giver and not just the gift!" This spoke to me deeply! I suddenly saw that there was nothing more important than my personal relationship with and love for God! This new mindset transformed everything, and I began to see people the way God sees them—as individuals for whom Christ died. I now learned to love those who God loved—people!

The Bible says we should **speak the truth in love and with a faith that works by love!**

*[T]hat we should no longer be children, tossed to and fro and carried about with every wind of doctrine, by the trickery of men, in the cunning craftiness of deceitful plotting, but, **speaking the truth in love**, may grow up in all things into Him who is the head – Christ.* Ephesians 4:14-15

*For we through the Spirit eagerly wait for the hope of righteousness by faith. For in Christ Jesus neither circumcision nor uncircumcision avails anything, but **faith working through love**.* Galatians 5:5-6

In the last days I am sure we shall all confront many challenges, even as Jesus said,

"These things I have spoken to you, that in Me you may have peace. In the world you will have tribulation; but be of good cheer, I have overcome the world." John 16:33

The Bible says we do not wrestle against flesh and blood but against principalities and powers of darkness; therefore, it is vital I establish my relationship of love with God to see things with His perspective. Jesus overcame the devil without losing His temper or being intimidated by the unbelief and mocking of those around Him. How do we respond under such intimidation?

Another prophecy for the last days says this:

And because lawlessness will abound, the love of many will grow cold. Matthew 24:12

Clearly, some people appear to have insufficient love to overcome the evil in the world. Could it be that their personal love for God was lacking? Was their personal relationship with God not a priority?

> *Love suffers long and is kind; love does not envy; … does not seek its own, is not provoked, thinks no evil; does not rejoice in iniquity, but rejoices in the truth; bears all things, believes all things, hopes all things, **endures all things. Love never fails**…* 1 Corinthians 13:4-8

Jesus' love was for the Father's will, rather than going His own way; and His obedience and devotion to doing the Father's will constrained him when under the greatest of provocation and temptation!

> *Finally, my brethren, be strong in the Lord and in the power of His might. Put on the whole armor of God, that you may be able to stand against the wiles of the devil. **For we do not wrestle against flesh and blood, but against principalities, against powers, against the rulers of the darkness of this age, against spiritual hosts of wickedness in the heavenly places.** Therefore take up the whole armor of God, that you may be able to withstand in the evil day, and having done all, to stand.* Ephesians 6:10-13

LIFE APPLICATIONS

- To live a true biblical life on this earth is going to increasingly require more of God's great agapé love and power!

- The Bible talks a lot about "overcoming." Ask yourself whether this a familiar word that is relevant to you.

THOUGHT

*And they **overcame** him by the blood of the Lamb and by the word of their testimony, and they did not love their lives to the death.*

Revelation 12:11

PART 4

DAY 28

Living in the Last Days —
To Stand: The Shield of Faith

Finally, my brethren, be strong in the Lord and in the power of His might. Put on the whole armor of God, that you may be able to stand against the wiles of the devil. For we do not wrestle against flesh and blood, but against principalities, against powers, against the rulers of the darkness of this age, against spiritual hosts of wickedness in the heavenly places. Therefore take up the whole armor of God, that you may be able to withstand in the evil day, and having done all, to stand.

Ephesians 6:10-13

Here we see that the true battle is not against fellow mankind but against the devil! That does not mean we should lower our guard with people—the devil uses people even though they may be oblivious to it! Anyone who denies Christ publicly and who speaks contrary to His Word is a potential instrument of the enemy! Remember! Man, through his corrupt, rebellious human nature, is a fallen being under the power and control of the devil and his angels.

Our attitude, therefore, as children of God, is that we are in the world but not of the world, having been born again into God's kingdom! Being born again is a hallmark of distinction between people. I have met people for the very first time and, within seconds, been in perfect unity with them! Why is this? Because we have both experienced the same saving grace of God in Jesus Christ and have been born again of His Spirit!

Remember, in the judgment we shall all stand before Jesus Christ to give account of our stewardship of what He has given us. Even our best and most faithful friends will not stand with us in that day! Therefore, our ultimate allegiance is to God! He loves us and will NEVER let us down!

The Scriptures below, together with Ephesians 6:10-13, are probably some of the most constructive, illuminating and detailed passages in the whole of the New Testament regarding spiritual warfare.

Stand therefore, having girded your waist with truth, having put on the breastplate of righteousness, and having shod your feet with the preparation of the gospel of peace; **above all, taking the shield of faith with which you will be able to quench all the fiery darts of the wicked one.** *And take the helmet of salvation, and the sword of the Spirit, which is the word of God; praying always with all prayer and supplication in the Spirit, being watchful to this end with all perseverance and supplication for all the saints.*

Ephesians 6:14-18

The devil is an expert at throwing his fiery darts of condemnation, accusation, and doubt at God's children. Faith in the written Word of God is stated here as our shield.

Remember the temptation of Jesus in the wilderness? Jesus used the greatest authority against the devil, to which he had no answer — the written Word of God. You see, the devil knows God's authority is the Word of God, the supreme power over all, and he will try to get around it somehow. The only way he can do this is to get us to doubt God's Word. Remember his menacing "sowing of doubt" strategy in the garden of Eden? – "Has God said?"

This is where the SHIELD OF FAITH comes in! It is my defence against all the accusations of the powers of darkness. I assert and proclaim God's Word!

The Bible puts it like this –

> *… Resist the devil and he will flee from you.*
>
> James 4:7

Yes! Even we human mortals can withstand the enemy using this shield, if we recognise and believe in the power and authority of God's Word! Why? Because He is our righteousness, and God gives us the shield of faith to defend ourselves against any spirit that seeks to tell us otherwise! We have been bought with a price — the blood of Christ! We are not our own! We belong to Him.

This is our stance against the enemy. The Blood of Christ is the guarantee of our position in Him, and it is the whole basis of our trust and faith in His Word. This truth will counter the devil's accusations against us regarding our unworthiness. Christ has died for us and redeemed us to Himself! That is the truth!

The devil will often come, seeking to sow doubt and accuse us, inferring that we are not good enough. And this is, of course, in a sense true — that is, by our own merit and righteousness, we all fall below God's standard, as it is written:

> *[F]or all have sinned and fall short of the glory of God.*
>
> Romans 3:23

But God's Word also says this:

There is therefore now NO CONDEMNATION to those who are in Christ Jesus…   Romans 8:1

… If God is for us, who can be against us?
                                      Romans 8:31

… It is God who justifies. Who is he who condemns? It is Christ who died…   Romans 8:33-34

I quite confidently tell the enemy that, in part, he is right. "I am, of myself, not good enough, BUT Jesus has paid the price in His own blood! Of myself, I am not righteous, but He has made me acceptable and right with God. I have given my life to Jesus Christ; I choose to believe, serve and obey Him!"

You can boldly assert, "I am the righteousness of God in Christ!"

The enemy has no power at all to do anything; he will go away. He cannot gainsay your choice to believe in Christ! He has **no** power over you as you declare your position in Christ according to the Word of God.

In the garden of Eden, this was the choice before Adam and Eve — to believe what God said or to believe what the serpent said.

The time has come to declare that we believe what GOD HAS SAID! This is our SHIELD OF FAITH! As you declare your trust in the Word of God, Satan has NO POWER OVER YOU!

The application of the shield of faith, at any given instant or circumstance, is to remember, speak or think of the written Word of God to combat against any onslaught of the enemy. As Jesus was accused and tempted, He immediately called to mind what was "written," and spoke this out in defence. It worked because, as already mentioned, the devil knows the authority of God's Word.

Remember, the Shield of Faith is given to you to use against the enemy. You do not argue with your own reasoning or intellect, because then you will always fail. The POWER is in the Word of God, the Sword of the Spirit! It is the only piece of armour that we use to attack; the rest of the armour is for our defence. That's how you get the victory, NEVER in yourself! All the arguments and discussions in the world will not protect you, but God's Word will.

Therefore, it is always good to familiarise yourself with God's Word every day. STUDY the Bible. LOVE it. ATTEND good Bible studies where the whole counsel of God is taught. And then... USE IT as a SHIELD and a SWORD against the enemy!

LIFE APPLICATIONS

- Thank you, Lord, for showing me the way to defeat the enemy; it is the very same way that You went!

- Thank you, Lord, for making me right with God. Help me to realise every day that it is only in Your righteousness that I can stand, and that it is not of myself.

- Lord, I come to trust in Your Word and take up my shield of defence to save me and deliver me from all accusations and doubts.

DAY 29

Living in the Last Days—
To Stand: The Sword of the Spirit

*And take... **the sword of the Spirit**, which is the word of God;*

Ephesians 6:17

As stated previously, the battle is not against flesh and blood but against invisible powers in a real, though invisible, sphere of activity. Paul, however, not only warns us of a clearly defined structure in the invisible realm; he instructs us to take up the whole armour of God to maintain a "battle stance" against this unseen evil structure. All this armour is not a passive protection in facing the enemy; it is to be used offensively against these Satanic forces.

Paul's final directive is in verse 18 instructing us to be:

...praying always with all prayer and supplication in the Spirit...

Thus, prayer is not so much a weapon, or even part of the armour; rather, it is how we engage in the battle itself and the purpose for which we are armed. To put on the armour of God is to prepare for battle. Prayer is the battle itself, with God's Word being the chief weapon employed against the enemy during our struggle.

For the word of God is living and powerful, and sharper than any two-edged sword, piercing even to the division of soul and spirit, and of joints and marrow, and is a discerner of the thoughts and intents of the heart. And there is no creature hidden from His sight, but all things are naked and open to the eyes of Him to whom we must give account.

Hebrews 4:12-13

Here we see that the Word of God is living and powerful and can determine whether a person is living a soulish or spiritual life! It is also clearly displayed in this context as a weapon against the adversary who, as we have said, cannot gainsay its authority — hence, it is powerful!

We will need to accept and understand the power and authority of God's Word by faith — basically, if God says it, it is done! If I believe in this authority behind the spoken Word, then equally it will be done for me also!

Before us, in the Bible, we see a book or rather many books whose words were written down by holy men of God as the Holy Spirit inspired them! The eyes of faith see well beyond the written letter of the page and recognise that these are the very words and thoughts of God Himself but written down in a form totally inspired by Him for our sake, that through them we might come to know Him and His power working in our lives.

The Bible is unique among all books in this respect, and it is only as we move into this realm of faith regarding what has been written — that is, by believing and receiving the Word — that we experience its authenticity, power, and authority in our personal lives.

The Spirit of God uses the Word of God as a weapon, called the Sword of the Spirit. When the very words written down in the Bible that we affirm and speak out by faith become endorsed and infused by the Spirit, He acts upon the spoken Word with His own indisputable sovereign power, bringing it to life with miraculous results. It is through this engagement with the Sword of the Spirit that we are able to perform spiritual warfare against the enemy. This, together with prayer, accomplishes those things that only God can do. As it is written:

*My word be that goes forth from My mouth; It shall not return to Me void, But **it shall accomplish what I please**, And it shall prosper in the thing for which I sent it.*
Isaiah 55:11

…'Not by might nor by power, but by My Spirit,' Says the Lord of hosts.
Zechariah 4:6

As you trust and believe God's Word, nothing can withstand it or come against you. Just as the devil left Jesus alone in the wilderness, not being able to gainsay the Word He spoke out against him, so the devil will leave you alone too.

*"**No weapon formed against you shall prosper**, And every tongue which rises against you in judgment You shall condemn. This is the heritage of the servants of the Lord, And their righteousness is from Me," Says the Lord.*
Isaiah 54:17

*… When the enemy comes in like a flood, **The Spirit of the Lord will lift up a standard against him.**"*

Isaiah 59:19

What we are discovering from the Bible in the above Scriptures is simply this: God acts upon His Word! Against the enemy, it is a sword. But remember, to a repentant sinner, it is the reconciling Word of grace!

LIFE APPLICATIONS

- To trust in the Lord is to trust in His Word.

- To love the Lord is to love and keep His Word.

A PRAYER

*Lord, I believe there are life-changing implications
whenever I speak your Word.
Teach me to exercise faith by trusting in the miraculous
power of Your Word over life's seemingly impossible
situations.*

DAY 30

Living in the Last Days — An Ambassador

*[A]nd for me, that utterance may be given to me, that I may open my mouth boldly to make known the mystery of the gospel, for which **I am an ambassador** in chains; that in it I may speak boldly, as I ought to speak.*   Ephesians 6:19-20

An ambassador is a diplomat or official who represents a country abroad. Their responsibility is to "represent" that country. This is their office: to speak not their own views or opinions but those of the country they represent. Consequently, an ambassador must be of mature stature, able to rightly present all that is required of them, being willing to speak and convey whatever they are asked to do.

Paul asks for prayer that he may speak boldly as he ought to speak. His sole desire is to be faithful to his office — an ambassador of Christ, preaching the Gospel! In his chains and imprisonment, he would constantly be chastised and probably beaten if ever he spoke of Jesus and "The Way" to others, but Paul's mission was to do exactly that. And he was determined to be faithful until the end! In this respect, the inward chains he wore in utter devotion to His Master were even greater than the physical chains that bound him. Paul repeatedly expressed his desire to fulfil His Master's call –

*[A]nd for me, that utterance may be given to me, **that I may open my mouth boldly**... that in it **I may speak boldly, as I ought to speak.***

Living in the last days as a child of the Living God will require this kind of attitude and faithfulness.

I need to be an ambassador of Christ! To speak not my own views or opinions upon any biblical matter but rather to proclaim precisely what is written! In answer to any question put forward to me when a person asks of my opinion, whether sincerely or otherwise, I must remember that an ambassador of Christ would always point people to the written Word of God. This places me outside of the picture, fulfilling the "office" of a true ambassador of Christ.

*For Christ did not send me to baptize, but to preach the gospel, **not with wisdom of words, lest the cross of Christ should be made of no effect.***

1 Corinthians 1:17

Here is a good example of where Paul exhibits the true role of an ambassador. He knew that men of his age, usually religious people and philosophers, often used worldly wisdom in their arguments to dispute the truth and testimony of our Lord Jesus Christ, seeking to belittle the teaching. Times have not changed! Paul declared this openly:

For the message of the cross is foolishness to those who are perishing, but to us who are being saved it is the power of God.   1 Corinthians 1:18

For since, in the wisdom of God, the world through wisdom did not know God, it pleased God through the foolishness of the message preached to save those who believe.

1 Corinthians 1:21

It is understood that we should always be faithful to our Lord and declare the truth of the Word of God to any enquiring ears. Whether it is accepted or rejected is not primarily our concern. If we have spoken the truth in love, as the Bible requires, peaceably and without malice, we have done what is required.

A declaration of one's testimony is also very powerful, for that can never be disputed; you have experienced certain thing for yourself, and therefore your words cannot be gainsaid!

*And I, brethren, when I came to you, **did not come with excellence of speech or of wisdom** declaring to you the testimony of God. **For I determined not to know anything among you except Jesus Christ and Him crucified.** I was with you in weakness, in fear, and in much trembling. **And my speech and my preaching were not with persuasive words of human wisdom**, but in demonstration of the Spirit and of power, that your faith should not be in the wisdom of men but in the power of God.*

1 Corinthians 2:1-5

Paul's declaration here is as bold as it is true! Notice how Paul declares the way he came to them:

"I was with you in weakness, in fear, and in much trembling."

Paul was in fear of his life constantly, and this predicament did not make him immune to human feelings and emotions. Yet, despite this, he did not waver in his commitment to Christ, and persecution intensified his demeanour even more. In his weakness, he asked for prayer to speak boldly; he remembered the words of the Lord spoken to him before:

*And He said to me, **"My grace is sufficient for you, for My strength is made perfect in weakness."** Therefore most gladly I will rather boast in my infirmities, that the power of Christ may rest upon me. Therefore I take pleasure in infirmities, in reproaches, in needs, in persecutions, in distresses, for Christ's sake. **For when I am weak, then I am strong.***   2 Corinthians 12:9-10

LIFE APPLICATIONS

- Jesus is called *the faithful witness* in Revelation 1:5 because He faithfully spoke the words of His Father, whether people welcomed them or not. Faithfulness is a very high quality in the Kingdom of God. Jesus will one day say to the faithful:

  'Well done, good and faithful servant; you were faithful over a few things, I will make you ruler over many things. Enter into the joy of your lord.'

- Paul needed to ask for prayer that he might remain faithful to speaking God's Word boldly.

  [A]nd for me, that utterance may be given to me, that I may open my mouth boldly… that in it I may speak boldly, as I ought to speak.

A PRAYER

Lord, help and strengthen me by the Power of the Holy Spirit to speak your Word boldly without fear.

DAY 31

Living in the Last Days — A Servant

He who loves his life will lose it, and he who hates his life in this world will keep it for eternal life. **If anyone serves Me, let him follow Me; and where I am, there My servant will be also. If anyone serves Me, him My Father will honour.** John 12:25-26

"He who loves his life will lose it." This statement refers to those who selfishly pursue their own agenda in life, living for immediate gratification, and whose priority is wealth and pleasure. They have no real regard for God and the purposes of His Kingdom, and seek to indulge themselves in the riches and pleasures of this life only.

"He who hates his life in this world will keep it for eternal life." This statement reveals the opposite. These are they who choose the purposes of God in this life as priority over their personal ambition and gain, recognising that this world will pass away but God's Kingdom will last forever. Like all people, they desire a degree of fulfilment and pleasure, but these will seek first the Kingdom of God above everything else and are prepared to sacrifice their own choices and desires for those of the Kingdom. This is the difference.

Jesus spoke plainly to His disciples in ways that would constitute great challenges in today's moderate and liberal society.

God's love incorporates in its very nature and essence the qualities of a servant. The mindset of the world rejects this outrightly — and will never accept it. A servant is, by very nature, a person who acknowledges and accepts a secondary position or rank to those whom they serve. They are willing to sacrifice all of the world's social standing regarding their rights.

Servants are usually attributed with duties and tasks that are considered to be mundane for a master to have to perform. Yet, Jesus says that those who will follow Him and serve Him will be highly favoured and blessed by God, their Father.

"If anyone serves Me, him My Father will honour."

Here is another vivid declaration of our Lord Jesus regarding servanthood:

... *"You know that the rulers of the Gentiles lord it over them, and those who are great exercise authority over them. Yet it shall not be so among you; but whoever desires to become great among you, **let him be your servant**. And whoever desires to be first among you, **let him be your slave— just as the Son of Man did not come to be served, but to serve, and to give His life a ransom for many."***
Matthew 20:25-28

As already stated, the world system will never accept this unselfish mode of conduct and life, but this is the language of the Kingdom of Heaven in contrast to that of this world.

<u>Key Points that Qualify a Servant of God</u>

- **Servants of God cannot live to themselves; otherwise they are not servants.**

   ...none of us lives to himself, and no one dies to himself. For if we live, we live to the Lord; and if we die, we die to the Lord...   Romans 14:7

   *Flee sexual immorality. Every sin that a man does is outside the body, but he who commits sexual immorality sins against his own body. Or do you not know that your body is the temple of the Holy Spirit who is in you, whom you have from God, and **you are not your own? For you were bought at a price; therefore glorify God in your body and in your spirit, which are God's.***
                    1 Corinthians 6:18-20

   Contrary to popular opinion in the world — and very often within the "church" — the Bible here declares that we are not our own! We were bought with a price, the blood of Jesus, and both our body and our spirit are God's! We have been brought back to God as His own purchased possession!
   We must ask ourselves: just how far have we departed from God and His unchangeable Word? How far have we compromised to accommodate views and behaviour in the world by diluting the Word of God to make it more appeasing to sinful man?

- **Servants are always ready and waiting.**

Unto You I lift up my eyes, O You who dwell in the heavens. **Behold, as the eyes of servants look to the hand of their masters, As the eyes of a maid to the hand of her mistress, So our eyes look to the Lord our God***...*   Psalm 123:1-2

Here I see a picture of a waiter or waitress in a restaurant, serving the needs of their customers. They are ready, waiting, looking, observing — eager to make themselves available to serve! This is a good parallel to serving God, for in doing so, are we not serving the needs of others?

- **True and faithful servants love their master, and their service reflects this.**

The Old Testament law governing servants is a wonderful example of servants who loves their master and desire to serve him forever and not go out free!

If you buy a Hebrew servant, he shall serve six years; and in the seventh he shall go out free and pay nothing... But if the servant plainly says, **'I love my master, my wife, and my children; I will not go out free,'** *then his master shall bring him to the judges. He shall also bring him to the door, or to the doorpost, and his master shall pierce his ear with an awl; and he shall serve him forever.*
                                     Exodus 21:2, 5-6

The very fact that the law made provision for this is interesting! Clearly this passage points to the bond of love between the servant of God and their Lord.

"If you love me," said Jesus, "Keep my commandments."

God is only interested in a bond of love with His people. Oh that we might recognise this, turn from our own way and surrender our all to Him!

Seek the Lord while He may be found,
Call upon Him while He is near.
Let the wicked forsake his way,
And the unrighteous man his thoughts;
Let him return to the Lord,
And He will have mercy on him;
And to our God,
For He will abundantly pardon.

Isaiah 55:6-7

LIFE APPLICATIONS

- The life of Jesus, as revealed in the Scriptures, shows us a totally different way of life, quite foreign to this world. A life that is: just, unselfish, obedient, humble, gracious, loving, kind, loving righteousness, hating sin…

A PRAYER

I come to You today, Lord, to humble myself and walk as Your servant in this world.

REFERENCES

i.   "In Tenderness He Sought Me" by W. Spencer Walton. © Public Domain.

ii.   "Amazing Grace" by John Newton. © Public Domain.

iii.   "This World Is Not My Home" by Albert E. Brumley. © 1937, Ren. 1965 Albert E. Brumley & Sons.

iv.   "Where Jesus Is, Tis Heaven" by Charles F. Butler. © Public Domain.

MY TESTIMONY

At the age of nineteen I was living at home with my parents in a place called Langwith Junction in Derbyshire, England which, as the name suggests, was a railway junction with sheds full of steam engines. It was a small village about one mile away from Shirebrook, a coal-mining market town.

By now I was well into university studies at Chelsea College of Science, London, and I always looked forward to coming home during vacation times to see my then girlfriend, Pauline Marchant, who lived about seven miles away in Mansfield. She was awesome, and I considered myself very lucky! It was during one Easter vacation in the year 1966 that I was ill in bed with the flu at my mum's house. I remember feeling quite low. My mother asked me to come to church with her as she said I would feel much better if I did. Being a dark cold Wednesday evening, I reluctantly yielded to her pressure, feeling I had no option but to go. "At least," I thought, "it is dark outside, and no one will particularly see me and where I am going!" You see, I felt stupid and embarrassed going to a church.

Upon arrival at a medium-sized Pentecostal Church Hall in Shirebrook, I saw no one there except two or three very elderly people—my mum had not told me it was a Prayer Meeting! To my utter amazement I recognised the man who stood at the front; it was Archie Roberts, and he owned a Fish and Chip shop in town!

I sat down sheepishly near the front feeling very conspicuous and downcast. Soon Archie began to preach, having read out a verse or two from the Bible.

He had read the passage from Matthew 16: 24-26 which went as follows:

"Then Jesus said to His disciples, "If anyone desires to come after Me, let him deny himself, and take up his cross, and follow Me. For whoever desires to save his life will lose it, but whoever loses his life for My sake will find it. For what profit is it to a man if he gains the whole world, and loses his own soul? Or what will a man give in exchange for his soul?"

He talked about man being born into this world naked, with nothing, and leaving it in a similar fashion. I was always inspired by truth, and this I could not dispute—it was true! As he went on about life, the Word began to speak to me—what would it profit me if I were to gain all the riches in the world only to die and then, that's it? I would leave everything behind! As a student I had plans to live a full life, hopefully with a good job, but this Word I was hearing shook me up to think more deeply and seriously. What was the meaning and purpose of my life? Where was I going? What was after? Being prompted by mum's elbow, I stood up at the end of the meeting to walk out to the front and be prayed for, giving my life to JESUS CHRIST.

I knew something spiritual had taken place that evening in the little hall; in fact, something supernatural! I had walked into the hall not knowing anything about God, but I walked out knowing this…

GOD was VERY REAL; I knew because, somehow, I had just met with HIM! Like I said, something spiritual happened; I don't know how—but it did!

From that day forward to this very day some fifty-two years later, God has been so real and personal to me.

I had once said mockingly to my mum that if God is real then He should talk with us and for that matter we with Him!

I instantly became hungry to read the Bible. I got to know Him more and more through His Word, which was opened up to me by His in-dwelling Holy Spirit!

He gave me what I was looking for—a purpose and reason for life, but most importantly, a real living relationship with God. I was not interested in religion but knowing God for myself—that was very different!

Now, I know this life is not the end but that it goes on with Him FOREVER!

Brian Reddish

2nd December 2017

All Books available in Print and e-book format.

Published by Caracal Books.

CONTACT THE AUTHOR

Email: brian@brianreddishbooks.uk

Website: www.brianreddishbooks.uk

www.ingramcontent.com/pod-product-compliance
Lightning Source LLC
Chambersburg PA
CBHW061103100726

47911CB00012B/369